FIVE LITTLE RICH GIRLS

FIVE
LITTLE
RICH
GIRLS

Lawrence Block

ALLISON & BUSBY
LONDON · NEW YORK

First published in Great Britain in 1984 by
Allison & Busby Ltd
6a Noel Street
London W1V 3RB
and distributed in the USA by
Schocken Books Inc.,
200 Madison Avenue
New York, NY 10016

Printing history:
Former title: *Make Out With Murder*
First published in paperback 1974 by Fawcett
Reprinted in paperback 1983 by Foul Play Press

British Library Cataloguing in Publication Data
Block, Lawrence
 Five little rich girls.
 I. Title
 813'.54[F]   PS3552.L63

ISBN 0 85031 545 X

Printed and bound in Great Britain by
Billings and Son Ltd, Worcester

for
KNOX BURGER
editor then, agent now
with respect, admiration and friendship
all in lieu of a commission

1

THE MAN WAS ABOUT FORTY OR FORTY-FIVE. I guessed his height at five-seven, which made him about four inches too short for his weight. He was wearing a brown suit, one of those doubleknit deals that are not supposed to wrinkle. His was sort of rumpled. He was wearing gleaming brown wing-tip shoes and chocolate brown socks. He wore a ring on his left pinky with what looked like a sapphire in it. Anyway, it was a blue stone, and I figure any blue stone is either a sapphire or trying to look like one.

I don't know all this because I have some kind of terrific memory or anything. I know it because I wrote it all down. Leo Haig says that ultimately I won't have to write things down in my notebook. He says I can train my memory to report all conversations verbatim and remember photographically what people are wearing and things like that. He says if Archie Goodwin can do it, so can I. It's a matter of training, he says.

Maybe he's right. I don't know. If so, I need all the training I can get. I figure it's going to be a good day if I remember in the morning where I put my wristwatch the night before.

Anyway, there's something we'd better get straight right in front. In the course of writing all this up for you, some of the facts will be as I've jotted them down in my notebook, and some will be as I happen to remember them, and things like conversations are as close as my memory can make them to how they happened originally. I don't have a tape recorder in my head, but I do tend to listen to people and remember not only what they said but how they said it. I suppose that's as close to the truth as you can generally come.

The guy in the brown suit was very boring to follow. I picked him up outside of the Gaily Gaily Theater on Eighth Avenue between 45th and 46th. That was 1:37 in the afternoon, and the particular afternoon was the third Wednesday in August. He emerged from the theater (*All-Male Cast! XXX-rated! Adults Only Positively!*) making those hesitant eye movements that you would expect anybody to make under those circumstances, as if he wanted to make sure that nobody he knew was watching him, but without making it obvious that he was looking around.

I picked him up because I liked the idea that he was already behaving with suspicion. It seemed likely that he would be more of a challenge.

See, I had no real reason to follow this man in particular. This was what Leo Haig calls a training exercise. We didn't have a case at the time, and while he enjoyed having me hang around and listen to him talk while he played with his tropical fish, we both eventually felt guilty if I wasn't doing something to earn the salary he paid me. So he sent me out to follow people. I would do this for as many hours as I could stand, and then I would go back and type up a report on my activities as a shadow. He would then read the report very critically. (I'm surprised he managed to read these reports at all, to tell you the truth. When all you do is follow a woman from her apartment building to Gristede's and back again, there is not a hell of a lot of excitement in a detailed report of what you have seen.)

But all of this would develop my powers of observation, he said, plus my skills in following people, in case we got a case that demanded that sort of thing. And it would also point up my journalistic talents. Leo Haig is very firm on this last subject, incidentally. It's not enough to be a great detective, he says, unless somebody writes about it well enough to let the world know about you.

Well, the guy in the brown suit certainly moved around enough. From the theater he went to a cafeteria on Broadway and had a cup of coffee and a prune Danish. I sat half a dozen tables away and pretended to drink my iced tea. He left the cafeteria and walked around the corner onto 42nd Street, where he entered First Amendment Books, a hole-in-the-wall that specializes in reading matter that abuses the amendment it's

8

named after. I don't know what he bought there because I didn't want to go in there after him. I loitered outside, trying not to look like a male hustler. By concentrating on Melanie Trelawney, I figured it might be easier to project a determinedly heterosexual image.

Thinking about Melanie Trelawney may not have made me *look* more heterosexual, but it certainly made me *feel* heterosexual as all hell. And thinking about Melanie came fairly easily to me because I had been thinking of very little else for the past month. In a sense, thinking about Melanie was more rewarding than spending time with her, because I allowed myself to play a more active role in thought than I did in life itself.

In the little plays I acted out in my head, for example, Melanie did not deliver lines like, "I think we should wait until we know each other better, Chip." Or, "I'm just not sure I'm stable enough for an active sexual relationship." Or, "Stop!"

My mental Melanie, my liberated, receptive Melanie was purring like a kitten while I stroked the soft skin of her upper thigh, when the man in the brown suit picked that moment to emerge from First Amendment with a parcel under his arm. Magazines, by the size and shape of the parcel. I had a fair idea what kind of magazines they were.

He headed west and walked briskly to Eighth Avenue. Just before he reached the corner he stopped in a doorway and talked to a tall slender young man wearing faded jeans and brand-new cowboy boots. They talked for a few moments and evidently failed to come to an agreement. My target heaved his shoulders and lurched away, and the kid with the boots gave him the finger.

On the other side of Eighth he had better luck. He stopped again in a doorway, and I loitered as unobtrusively as possible while they got it together. Then they walked side by side over to Ninth Avenue and two blocks north to something that was supposed to be a hotel. That's what the sign said, anyhow. From the looks of it I got the feeling that if you ever needed a cockroach in a hurry, that was the place to look for one.

There was a liquor store next to the hotel, and they stopped there first, with the hustler waiting outside while Brown Suit bought a bottle. He came out with a pint of something and they went into the hotel together.

I was going to leave him there and say the hell with it, and either follow somebody else or call it a day, but Haig had told me just a couple of days ago that the attribute of a successful surveillance man most difficult to develop was patience. "You must cultivate *sitzfleisch*, Chip. Sitting flesh. A mark of professionalism is the ability to do absolutely nothing when to do otherwise would be an improper course of action."

I went into the coffee shop across the street and settled my *sitzfleisch* on a wobbly counter stool. The special of the day was meat loaf, which suggested that the activity of the night before had been sweeping the floor. I had a glazed doughnut and a lot of weak coffee, and concentrated on developing the ability to do absolutely nothing.

While I worked on this I did a little more thinking about Melanie Trelawney.

I had met her a month ago. I was in Tompkins Square Park trying to decide whether or not I wanted a Good Humor. The Special Flavor of the Month was Chocolate Pastrami and I wasn't sure I could handle it, but it did sound off the beaten track. Somebody came by that I knew, and then someone else materialized with a guitar, and eventually a batch of us were sitting around singing songs of social significance. After a while somebody started passing out home-made cigarettes with an organic and non-carcinogenic tobacco substitute in them, but I just passed them up, because by this time I had seen Melanie and I was high already.

We got to talking. Nine times out of ten when I meet a really sensational girl it takes an exchange of perhaps fourteen sentences before one or both of us realizes we could easily bore each other to death. Sometimes, say one time in ten, it doesn't happen that way. In which case I tend to flip out a little.

I'll tell you something. Sometimes when two people meet each other, the best thing that can happen is that they go directly to the nearest bed. Other times the best thing can

10

happen is that they take their time and really get to know each other first. Either way is cool. The problem comes when the two people perceive the situation differently.

Not that she was precisely driving me up a wall. There were times when it felt that way, I'll admit, but basically it was a question of Melanie's feeling it was very necessary for us to take our time, while I felt that all the time we had to take was whatever time it took to get out of our clothes. Since Melanie always wore jeans and tie-dyed top and sandals, and nothing under any of those three articles of clothing but her own sweet self, and since I was sufficiently motivated to take off my shirt without unbuttoning it, this process would not have taken much time.

It probably wasn't as bad as I'm making it sound. I mean, I'm not Stanley Stud who has to have a woman every night or his thing will turn green. I *want* a woman every night, but I've learned to live with failure. We were getting to know each other, Melanie and I, and we were getting to know each other slightly in a physical way, and eventually things were going to work out. Until then I wasn't sleeping very well, but I had decided I could put up with that.

I sat at the counter and stirred my coffee, trying to convince myself that I wanted to drink it. Every few seconds I would glance out through the window to see if the man in the brown suit was finished and ready to lead me off to still more exciting places. Every once in a while someone with the same general orientation as Brown Suit would give me a sidelong glance. Which made me think defensively again of Melanie.

One thing had been bothering me lately. I couldn't escape the feeling that Melanie might be a little bit out of touch with reality.

For maybe the past ten days she had been behaving strangely. She would laugh suddenly at nothing at all, and then a few minutes later she would start crying and not say what it was about. And then a couple of days earlier she explained what it was. She was convinced she was going to die.

"Two of my sisters are already gone," she said. "First Robin was killed in a car accident. Then Jessica threw herself out of the window. There's just three of us left, Caitlin and Kim and me, and then we'll all be gone."

"In seventy years, maybe. But not like tomorrow, Melanie."

"Maybe tomorrow, Chip."

"I think maybe you do drugs a little too much."

"It's not drugs. Anyway, I'm straight now."

"Then I don't get it."

Her eyes, which range from blue to green and back again, were a very vivid blue now. "I am going to be killed," she said. "I can sense it."

"What do you mean?"

"Just what I said. Robin and Jessica were killed—"

"Well, Jessica killed herself, didn't she?"

"Did she?"

"Jesus, Melanie, that's what you just said, isn't it? You said she threw herself out a window."

"Maybe she did. Maybe she . . . she was pushed."

"Oh, wow!"

She lowered her head, closed her eyes. "Oh, I don't know what I'm talking about. I don't know anything, Chip. All I know is the feelings I've had lately. That all of the Trelawney girls are going to die and that I'm going to be next. Maybe Robin's accident really was an accident. Maybe Jessica did kill herself. She wasn't terribly stable, she had a weird life style. And maybe Robin's accident really was an accident. I know it must have been. But—I'm *afraid*, Chip."

I saw her a couple of times after that, and she was never that hysterical again. She did mention the subject, though. She tried to be cool about it.

"Well, like it's a good thing you're working for a private detective, Chip. That way you can investigate the case when I'm murdered."

I would tell her to cut the shit, that she was not going to be murdered, and she would say she was just making a joke out of it. Except it was only partly a joke.

I guess that coffee shop wasn't the best place to pick for a stake-out. Not just because the coffee was rotten, but because the clientele was largely gay.

12

Which is all right as far as I'm concerned. I don't get uncomfortable in homosexual company. I have a couple of gay friends, as far as that goes. But the thing is this: if you sit in a place like that, just killing time over a cup of coffee, and if you're young and tallish and thinnish, which is to say the general physical type which is likely to hang out in such a place for a particular purpose, well, people come to an obvious conclusion.

It was getting a little heavy, so I paid for my coffee and went out to wait outside. I guess that turned out to be worse. I wasn't outside for five minutes before a heavy-set man with a slim attaché case and a neatly trimmed white mustache asked me if he could buy me a drink.

I took my wallet out and flipped it open briefly. "Police," I said. "Surveillance," I said. "Scram," I said.

"Oh dear," the man said.

"Just go away," I said.

"I didn't actually do anything," the man said. "Just an offer of a drink, all in good faith—"

"Jesus, go away," I said.

"I'm not under arrest?"

Across the street, the man in the brown suit emerged from the hotel. He still had his package of magazines with him. I told the idiot with the mustache that he was not under arrest, but that he would be if he didn't piss off.

"You're not Vice Squad?"

"Narcotics," I said, trying to get past him.

"But you should be on Vice Squad," he insisted. "You'd fool anyone."

I've decided since that he must have intended this as a compliment. At the time I couldn't pay that much attention to what he was saying because Brown Suit was on his way into a subway kiosk and I had to hurry if I didn't want to lose him. It occurred to me that perhaps I did want to lose him, but I wanted to get away from the creep with the mustache in any case, so I charged down to the subway entrance and caught sight of the man in brown just as I dropped my own token into the turnstile. Actually, it was his turn to follow me for the next little bit, because he had to buy a token. I always have a pocket

13

full of them. Leo Haig believes his right-hand man should be prepared for any contingency.

I bought a paper to give myself something to hide behind and to kill time so that he could let me know which train we were going to ride. It turned out to be the downtown A train and we rode it to Washington Square. Then we went up and around and caught the E train as far as Long Island City. This puzzled me a little because he could have caught that same E train at 42nd Street and saved going out of the way a couple of miles, but I figured maybe he changed his mind and had some particular last-minute reason to go out to Queens.

At Long Island City he got out of the train just as the doors were closing, and if I hadn't been standing right next to the door at the time I would have gone on riding to Flushing or someplace weird like that. But I got out, and I immediately began walking off in the opposite direction from him. After I had gone about twenty yards I turned and looked over my shoulder and there he was. I started to turn again, but he was making motions with his hands.

I just stood there. I didn't really know what else to do.

"Look," he said. "This is beginning to get on my nerves."

"Huh?"

"You've been following me all afternoon, son. Would you like to tell me why?"

Leo Haig always tells me to use my instinct, guided by my experience. He stole this bit of advice from Nero Wolfe. My problem is, I haven't had too much experience and my instincts aren't always that razor-sharp.

But what I said was, "I have to say something to you."

"Well, you could have said it back on Ninth Avenue, son. You didn't have to wait until we both rode back and forth underneath Manhattan Island."

"The thing is, I don't know if you're the right man."

"What right man?"

"The married man who's been running around with my sister, and if you are—"

Well, he damned well wasn't, and that was a load off both our minds. He laughed a lot, and he did everything but explain

14

to me precisely why he was extremely unlikely to be running around with anybody's sister, or to be married, and we went our separate ways to our mutual relief. I got another E train heading back in the direction I'd come from and he went somewhere else.

At least he hadn't made me until I'd tailed him to Ninth Avenue. I suppose that was something.

There's probably a good way to connect from the E train to something that goes somewhere near the Lower East Side, but I'm still not brilliant about the subway system and the maps they have there are impossible to figure out, especially when the train is (a) moving and (b) crowded, which this one certainly was. So I rode down to Washington Square again, feeling a little foolish about the whole thing, and then I got out and walked cross-town. I called Melanie a couple of times en route, but the line was busy.

Melanie's place was on Fifth Street between Avenue C and Avenue D. I could never figure out why. I mean, I could figure out why the building was there. It had no choice. Buildings tend to stay where you put them, and nobody would have allowed this building in a decent neighborhood anyway. But Melanie did have a choice. She wasn't wildly rich, and I don't suppose she could have stayed at the Sherry-Netherland, but she could have had a better apartment in a safer neighborhood with the income she got from her father's estate. Instead she lived on one of the most squalid and unsafe blocks in the city.

"You know," I'd told her a day or two ago, "if you really insist on having this irrational fear of being murdered, you ought to move out of this rathole. Because when you live here, being murdered isn't an irrational fear. It's a damned rational one."

"I feel secure here," she said.

"The streets are wall-to-wall junkies and perverts," I said. "The muggers have their own assigned territories so they don't mug each other by mistake. What makes you feel secure?"

"It's a settled neighborhood, Chip."

I walked through it now. It was at its very worst in the afternoon because the light was bright enough to see how grungy it was. It was also bright in the morning, but there was no one around. Starting a little after noon, the rats would begin to peep out of their holes.

I got to her building. They still hadn't replaced the front door. No one knew who had taken it, or why. I walked up four very steep flights of stairs and knocked on her door.

There was no answer.

I knocked a couple more times, called her name a lot, and then tried the door. It was locked, and that worried me.

See, Melanie would only lock her door when she was home. I know most people do it the other way around, or else lock it all the time, but she had a theory on the subject. If a junkie burglar knew she wasn't home, and found the door locked, he would simply kick it in. This would mean she would have to pay for a new lock. If, however, she left it unlocked, he would come in, discover there was nothing around to take, and finally settle for ripping off her radio. Since the radio had cost fifteen dollars and the big cylinder lock had cost forty, it was clear where the priorities lay.

I knocked again, a lot louder. She would not be asleep at this hour. And her telephone had been busy just a few minutes ago. Of course telephones in New York are capable of being busy just for the hell of it, but—

I got this sudden flash and didn't like it at all. So I did something I've wanted to do for years. I think it's something everybody secretly wants to do.

I kicked the door in.

You'd be surprised how easy that is. Or maybe you wouldn't when you stop to think that some of the most decrepit drug addicts in the world do it a couple of times a day. I hauled back and kicked with my heel, hitting the door right on the lock. On the third try the door flew open and the forty-dollar lock went flying, and I lost my balance and sat down without having planned to. I suppose a few tenants heard me do all these things, but they evidently knew better than to get involved.

The apartment was rabbit warren, a big living room and a long hallway that kept leading to other rooms, some of them containing Salvation Army reject furniture, some of them

16

papered with posters of Che and stuff like that. Actually I think Melanie paid as much rent for the place as I paid for a room in a decent neighborhood. She said she liked having plenty of space. Personally, considering the condition of the rooms, I would think that a person would pay more for less space. One room in that building would have been bad enough. Five rooms was ridiculous.

The telephone was in the living room. It was off the hook. I worked my way through the apartment, calling out her name, picking up more and more negative vibrations and getting less and less happy about the whole thing.

I found her in the back room. She was spread out stark naked on her air mattress, which is just how I had always hoped to find her.

But she was also absolutely dead, and that was not what I had had in mind at all.

2

SHE WASN'T THE FIRST CORPSE I HAD EVER SEEN. One summer I picked apples for a while in upstate New York, a job which consisted largely of falling off ladders. The other pickers would go out drinking when they were done, and sometimes I would tag along. There was usually at least one fight an evening. Sometimes somebody would pull a knife, and one time when this happened it wound up that one guy, a wiry man with a harelip, caught a knifeblade in his heart and died. I saw him when they carried him out.

The first book I wrote, I covered my experiences apple-picking, but never put that part in. God knows why.

So she wasn't the first corpse I ever looked at, but she might as well have been. I kept thinking how horrible it was that she looked so beautiful, even in death. Her pale white skin had a blue tint to it, especially in her face. Her eyes were wide open and I could swear they were staring at me.

I knew she was dead. No living eyes ever looked like that. But I had to reach down and touch her. I put one hand on her shoulder. She'd been dead long enough to grow cool, however long that takes. I don't know much about things like that. I'd never had to.

I almost didn't see the hypodermic needle. She was on her back, legs stretched out in front of her, one arm at her side, the other placed so that her hand was on her little bowl of a stomach. That hand almost covered the hypodermic needle. After I saw it, I picked up her other arm and found a needle mark. Just one, and it looked fresh.

I put her arm back the way I had found it. I went to the bathroom and threw up and came back and looked at her some more. I must have stood there staring at her for five minutes. Then I paced around the whole apartment for another five minutes and came back and stared at her some more.

This wasn't shock. I was in shock, of course, but I was being very methodical about this. I wanted to notice everything and I wanted to make sure I remembered whatever I noticed.

I left her apartment, closed the door, walked down the stairs and out. I walked all the way over to First Avenue before I caught a cab. The cab dropped me at 14th Street and Seventh. I walked quickly from there to my rooming house on 18th Street, a few doors west of Eighth.

When I was in my own room on the third floor, the first thing I did was lock the door. The second thing was to go into the bathroom and remove the towel bar from the wall. It's a hollow stainless steel bar, and there was a little plastic vial in it that contained several dollars' worth of reasonably good grass. I poured the grass in the toilet and flushed, rinsed out the vial, and tossed it out the window. Then I went through the medicine cabinet. I couldn't find anything to worry about except for a few codeine pills that my doctor had prescribed for a sinus headache. I thought about it and decided to hell with them, and I flushed them away, too. That left nothing but aspirin and Dristan, and I didn't think the cops would hassle me much for either of those. I put the towel bar back and washed my hands.

I looked in the mirror and decided I didn't like the way I was dressed. I put on a fresh shirt and a pair of slacks that didn't need pressing too badly. I traded in my loafers for my black dress shoes.

Then I went downstairs to the pay phone in the hall. I dropped a dime in the slot and dialed the number I know best.

Haig answered the telephone himself for a change. We talked for a few minutes. Mostly I talked and he listened, and then he made a couple of suggestions, and I hung up the phone and went off to discover the body.

I guess I'll have to tell you something about Leo Haig.

The place to start, I suppose, is how I happen to be working for him. I had been looking for a job for a while, and things had not been going particularly well. I got work from time to time, washing dishes or bussing tables or delivering messages and parcels, but none of these positions amounted to what you might call A Job With A Future, which is what I have always been seeking, though in a sort of inept way.

My problem, really, was that I wasn't qualified for anything too dynamic. My education stopped a couple of months before graduation from Upper Valley Preparatory Academy, which is to say that I haven't even got a high school diploma, for Pete's sake. And my previous work experience — well, when you tell a prospective employer that you have been an assistant to Gregor the Pavement Photographer, a termite salesman, a fruit picker, and a deputy sheriff in a whorehouse in South Carolina, well, what usually happens is his eyes glaze and he points at the door a lot.

(I don't want to go into all this ancient history now, really, but if you're interested you could read about it. My first two books, *No Score* and *Chip Harrison Scores Again*, pretty well cover the territory. I don't know that they're much good, but you could read them for background information or something. Assuming you care.)

Anyway, I was living in New York and doing the hand-to-mouth number and reading the want ads in *The Times*, and there were loads of opportunities to earn $40 a week if you had a doctorate in chemical engineering or something like that, but not much if you didn't. Then I ran into an ad that went something like this:

RESOURCEFUL YOUTH wanted to assist detective. Low pay, long hours, hard work, demanding employer. Journalistic experience will be given special consideration. Familiarity with tropical fish helpful but not absolutely necessary. An excellent opportunity for one man in a million....

I didn't know if I was one man in a million, but it was certainly one advertisement in a million, and nothing could have kept me from answering it. I called the number listed in the ad and answered a few questions over the phone. He gave me an address and I went to it, and at first I thought the whole thing was someone's idea of a joke, because the building was obviously a whorehouse. But it turned out that only the lower two floors were a whorehouse. The upper two floors were the office and living quarters of Leo Haig.

He wasn't what I expected. I don't know exactly what I expected, but whatever it might have been, he wasn't it. He's about five-two and very round. It's not that he's terribly heavy, just that the combination of his height and girth makes him look something like a beachball. He has a head of wiry black hair and a pointed black goatee with a few gray hairs in it. That beard is very important to him. I've never seen it when it was not trimmed and groomed to perfection. He touches it a lot, smoothing and shaping it. He says it's an aid to thought.

I spent three hours with him that first day, and at the end of the three hours I had a job. He spent the first hour pumping me, the second showing off his tropical fish, and the final hour talking about everything in the world, himself included. I went out of there with a lot more knowledge than I had brought with me, A Job With A Future, and a whole lot of uncertainty about the man I was working for. He was either a genius or a lunatic and I couldn't make up my mind which.

I still haven't got it all worked out. I mean, maybe the two are not mutually exclusive. Maybe he's a genius *and* a lunatic.

The thing is, the main reason I got the job was that I had had two books published. You may wonder what this has to do with being the assistant of a private detective. It's very simple, really. Leo Haig isn't content with being the world's greatest detective. He wants the world to know it.

"There are a handful of detectives whose names are household words," he told me. "Sherlock Holmes. Nero Wolfe. Their brilliance alone would not have guaranteed them fame. It took the efforts of other men to bring their deeds to public attention. Holmes had his Watson. Wolfe has his Archie Goodwin. If a detective is to make the big time, a trustworthy associate with literary talent is as much a prerequisite as a personality quirk and an eccentric hobby."

Here's something I have to explain to you if you are going to understand Leo Haig at all.

He believes Nero Wolfe exists.

He really believes this. He believes Wolfe exists in the brownstone, with the orchids and Theodore and Fritz and all the rest of it, and Archie Goodwin assists him and writes up the cases and publishes them under the pen name of Rex Stout.

"The most telling piece of evidence, Chip. Consider that *nom de plume*, if you will. And of course it's just that; no one was ever born with so contrived a name as Rex Stout. But let us examine it. Rex is the Latin for king, of course. As in *Oedipus Rex*. And Stout means, well, fat. Thus we have what? A fat king — and could one ask for a more perfect appellation to hang upon such an extraordinary example of corpulence and majesty as Nero Wolfe?"

Haig hasn't always been a detective. Actually he's only been a detective about a year longer than I've been an assistant detective. Until that time he lived in a two-room apartment in the Bronx and raised tropical fish to sell to local pet shops. This may strike you as a hard way to make a living. You'd be right. Most tropical fish are pretty inexpensive when you buy them from the pet shop, and even that price has to be three or four times what the shopkeeper pays for them, because he has to worry about a certain percentage of them dying before he can get them sold. Haig had developed a particularly good strain of velvet swordtails — the color was deeper than usual, or something — and he had a ready market for most of the other fish he raised as well, but he was not getting rich this way.

The way he got rich took relatively little effort on his part. His uncle died and left him $128,000.

As you can probably imagine, that made quite a difference in his life. Because all of a sudden he didn't have to run around New York with plastic bags full of little fishes for sale. He could do what he had always dreamed of doing. He could become the World's Greatest Detective.

Raising fish had been Leo Haig's only way to make a living, but it had not been his only interest. He has what is probably the largest library of mystery and detective fiction in the world. I think he has just about everything ever written on the subject.

22

The Nero Wolfe novels, from *Fer-De-Lance* to the latest one, are all in hard cover; after he received his inheritance he had them all rebound in hand-tooled leather. He's been reading all of these things since he was a kid, and he remembers what he reads. I mean, he can tell you not only the plot, but the names of all the characters in some Ngaio Marsh mystery that he read fifteen years ago. It's pretty impressive, let me tell you.

The house is pretty impressive, too, and he has emphasized that he wants me to write about the house, but I'll wait until I come to the part about going there and then I'll describe it for you. I'll just say now that he picked it when he had collected his inheritance and started to set up shop as a detective. He moved in with his books and fish tanks, he managed to get a license as a private investigator, he listed himself in the Yellow Pages, and he sat back and waited for the world to discover him.

The trouble is that he's too rich and he's not rich enough. If he had more money, like a couple of million, it wouldn't matter if he ever worked or not. If he had less money, like nothing substantial in the checking account, it would mean that he'd have to take the few cases that come his way. But he's got just enough money to let him maintain high standards. He won't touch divorce work, for example. He won't do any sort of snooping that requires electronic gear, which he regards as the handtools of the devil. And he won't accept anything routine. What he wants, really, is to handle nothing but baffling murder cases that he can solve through the exercise of his incredible brain, with the faithful Chip Harrison doing the legwork and writing up everything afterwards.

I know his secret hope. Someday, if he makes enough of a name for himself, if he keeps his standards high, develops just the right sort of eccentricities and idiosyncrasies, possibly someday Nero Wolfe will invite him over to the house on 35th Street for dinner.

That's really what he lives for.

I suppose my civic duty called upon me to phone the police as soon as I discovered Melanie's body. I'm glad I didn't let my civic duty interfere with my instinct for self-preservation,

23

because it turned out that Detective Gregorio took my towel bar off the wall and checked it out to see if I had drugs stashed in it. That was just about the first place he looked. I'm never keeping anything incriminating in there again, believe me. Pick a place that you figure is the last place the police would think of looking, and that's the *first* place they think of looking. It's the damnedest thing.

But I'm getting ahead of myself. What happened was, I went back to Melanie's place, figuring it was possible that the police had already found her without my help, but they hadn't. I had left a book on the floor so that it would be moved if anybody pushed the door more than a third of the way open, and it was still in its original position, so it seemed unlikely anybody had been in the apartment since I'd left it.

I went on inside, and I had an irrational hope that I had been somehow mistaken and Melanie would turn out to be alive after all, which is pretty stupid to write down and all, but impossible to avoid wishing at the time. Of course she was still there, and of course she was dead, and of course I felt sick all over again, but instead of throwing up any more I went into the living room and called 911.

The person who picked up the phone put me on HOLD before I had a chance to say anything, which would have been aggravating if I'd been bleeding to death or something, but then a couple of seconds later a cop came on the line and I gave him the story. They were fast enough after that. It was 5:18 when I placed the call and the first two patrolmen arrived at 5:31. You would have thought it would take them almost that long to climb the stairs. They spent most of their time walking around and opening drawers and telling me not to touch anything. They were basically waiting for the detectives but they didn't want it to look as though they were waiting for the detectives, so they asked me a lot of boring questions and sneaked a lot of peeks at Melanie's body. This seemed very disrespectful to me, but I didn't think they would care to hear my feelings on the matter so I kept them to myself.

The detectives got there before very long and took over. There was Detective Gregorio, whom I mentioned before, and his partner Detective Seidenwall. Gregorio is tall and dark and handsome, and he has one of those twenty-dollar haircuts, and he didn't like me much. Seidenwall is older, say fifty, and his name is easy to remember because he looks like the side of a wall, and he didn't like me at all.

They both seemed to despise me, to tell you the truth.

The trouble started with my name. They said they wanted a full name, not a nickname, and I explained that Chip was my legal first name, and eventually I had to show identification to prove it. They wanted to know what I was doing in Melanie's apartment and I said she was a friend and had invited me to stop in after work.

"Oh. you work, huh?" said Seidenwall.

"I work for Leo Haig. The detective."

"You mean some kind of private cop? You on some kind of a case?"

"No. Melanie was my friend."

"Uh-huh. You a junkie too?"

"Of course not."

"Roll up your sleeves, punk."

This struck me as silly, since I was wearing a short-sleeved shirt, but I rolled up what little sleeves I had. Gregorio got a little suspicious over a mosquito bite, but turned his attention to other things. He and Seidenwall asked me approximately seven million questions, many of them consisting of the same ones over again. How long had Melanie been a junkie? How long had I been sleeping with her? Had she died right away, or was it gradual?

This last question was a trap, of course. There were a lot of questions like this, designed to trick me into admitting I had been with her when she died. There were other trick questions, geared to establish that I had sold the heroin to her. They seemed to take it for granted that it was heroin, and she had died of an overdose of it.

The questions went on for a while. They probably would have asked me fewer questions if they hadn't hated me on sight, and they would have gone on hassling me longer except they were bored with the whole thing. It was all pretty obvious to them. Melanie had overdosed herself with heroin and that was why she was dead. When I pointed out that she had never to my knowledge been a drug addict, had never used a needle, they nodded without much enthusiasm and said that made an OD that much more likely. She wouldn't know about the proper dose, for one thing. And she would have had no time to build up a gradual tolerance to the drug. Finally, some people go into something called anaphylactic shock the first time they try certain substances. Penicillin, for some people. Or a bee sting, or heroin.

Anyway, she was dead, and as far as they were concerned it was an accidental drug-related homicide, and they got too many of them to be terribly interested in each new one that came along. So they asked me all their questions and took a short statement from me, and then they asked me for permission to accompany me to my own residence and search the premises, and of course I could have refused because they didn't have a warrant. But they already hated me enough for one day, I figured, and besides I had thrown away not only the illegal marijuana but the legal codeine tablets, so in a way I was almost glad they wanted to search my room. I mean, I'd have felt a little foolish if I had gone through all of that for nothing.

Gregorio and Seidenwall seemed unhappy when they didn't find anything. They held a whispered conversation by the bathroom door, and I caught enough of it to get an idea what it was about. Seidenwall wanted to plant some drugs so they would have an excuse to arrest me. Gregorio talked him out of it, not out of fondness to me, but because he felt I wasn't worth the trouble.

"I'll tell you, Harrison," he said on his way out. "You're the only thing in this that doesn't make sense. Everything else is pretty open and shut. But you don't figure."

"Why?"

"You swear it's not a business thing with the girl. That she's a friend. And then you tell us you've known her for a month and you weren't balling her."

"I wasn't."

"You a faggot?"

26

"No."

"Everybody knows those hippie chicks go like rabbits. It's what you call common knowledge. But you knew her for a month without getting in her pants. It don't add up."

I didn't say anything.

"Number two. You go to her apartment and find her dead with a needle in her arm." The needle was not in her arm, but I let it pass. "And what do you do? You call the cops."

"Isn't that what a person is supposed to do?"

"Of course it's what a person is supposed to do. Nobody in this fucking city does what he's supposed to do. Nobody wants to get involved. Nobody wants to call himself to the attention of the police, especially in a drug-related homicide, especially when the person in question is a hippie punk that probably uses drugs himself."

"I don't."

"Yeah, you don't. And you're not a hippie punk either, are you? You're some kind of a cop."

"I work—"

"Yeah, I know. You work for this Haig, who's some kind of private cop that I never heard of. You're his assistant. What do you assist him with?"

"Cases."

"Uh-huh. I'll tell you one thing, Harrison. I hope this Haig character looks more like a cop than you do. Because you just don't fit the image of a cop, Harrison. Private or otherwise, you're not my idea of a cop."

I pictured Leo Haig and tried to decide which of the two of us looked more like a cop. I gave up thinking about it because it made me feel like giggling and I didn't want to giggle. I had the feeling that one giggle from me was all Seidenwall would need.

I wasn't sleeping with Melanie, I had done my civic duty and called the police, and I didn't look like any kind of a cop. Those were the three things about me that made Gregorio and Seidenwall suspicious. I couldn't quite follow their reasoning on this, but then again I didn't have to.

Suspicious or not, they walked out my door and down the

27

stairs without even telling me not to leave town. So their suspicion was evidently just on general principles, coupled with instinctive dislike.

I suppose they would have given me a much worse time if they'd had the brains to realize Melanie had been murdered.

3

"IT WAS DEFINITELY MURDER," I said. "First of all, Melanie would never give herself a shot of heroin. She told me she tried heroin once, she snorted it, and it made her nauseous without giving her any kind of a high at all."

"She might try it a second time."

"She might, but there were too many other things she liked better. And if she did try it again, it wouldn't be with a needle. She's terrified of needles. Some nurse had to give her an injection once and botched it, kept stabbing around trying to find the vein, and she still has nightmares about it. Still *had* nightmares about it. Oh, shit."

"Settle yourself, Chip."

I nodded across the desk at him. It's what they call a partners' desk, with drawers and stuff on both sides so two people can use it. I was on my side of the desk. I was very flattered to have a whole side of a desk to myself, but I really didn't have much of anything to keep in the drawers.

Haig took a pipe out of a little wooden rack on his side of the desk. This was during his pipe period. He had trouble keeping them lit, and they kept burning his mouth. He was convinced that he would sooner or later break a pipe in, and sooner or later find a mild enough tobacco, but in the meantime he was doing his best. He thought pipe-smoking might be good for the image. He took the pipe apart and cleaned it while I settled myself. He never did get around to smoking it that night.

I said, "Another thing. Melanie was extremely careful about that air mattress. You had to take your shoes off before you sat on it, and she would make me check to see if I had anything sharp in my pockets. She was very nervous about puncturing the thing."

Haig nodded. "The syringe."

"Right. Even assuming she decides to take heroin, and even assuming she's going to shoot it, the last place in that apartment she'd pick to use a hypodermic needle is the air mattress."

"You didn't point this out to the police."

"No. I didn't point out anything to them, like telling them how she was afraid she was going to die."

"Perfectly within your rights." He touched his beard, stroked it with love and affection. "A citizen is under no compulsion to volunteer unrequested information to the police. He is merely obliged to answer their questions honestly and completely, and make no false statements."

"Well, I fell down there."

"The lock."

"Right. They asked how I got in and I told them the lock was wrecked a couple of weeks ago in a burglary and she hadn't got around to replacing it yet."

"And of course you didn't tell them you had been there once before."

"No. I, uh, more or less gave them the impression I spent the past four hours with you."

"I think that was wise," he said. "They should have noticed the syringe and the air mattress. That should have been as obvious as a third nostril." He closed his eyes for a moment and his hand worked on his beard. "You should have told me of Miss Trelawney's fear of death."

"What could you have done?"

"Probably nothing. Hmmm. There were five girls altogether, I understand. Five Misses Trelawney."

"That's right. And now three of them are dead."

"And two alive. Are the survivors living here in New York?"

"I don't know. I don't really know anything about them."

"Hmmmm. Perhaps you know more than you think. Melanie must have talked about them."

"Actually, she didn't talk too much about anything. She wasn't very verbal."

He nodded approvingly. "I've never felt loquacity is a mark of excellence in a woman. Nevertheless, she no doubt mentioned something about the girls who died. Their names, if nothing else."

30

"Robin and Jessica."

"One died in an auto wreck and the other fell from a window?"

"Yes. Let me think. Jessica went out the window and Robin died in the car accident."

He pursed his lips. At least he did something weird with his lips, and I have never quite known what it is that you do when you purse your lips, but this was probably it. "Let's not call it an accident, Chip," he said. "Let's merely call it a wreck, just as we'll say that Jessica fell from a window, not that she threw herself out."

"You think they were both murdered?"

"I think we ought to take it as a postulate for the time being. And we have to assume that whoever had a motive for murdering three of five sisters is not going to discontinue his activities before he has done for the remaining two into the bargain. Which of the sisters was the first to die?"

I had to think. "Robin first, then Jessica. I don't know about the timing, though. All of this happened before I met Melanie. I have the impression that Jessica died two or three months ago, but I really don't know how long before then Robin died."

He closed his eyes. "That's very interesting," he said.

"What is?"

"First an auto wreck," he said. "Then a fall, then an overdose of heroin. Assuming that an autopsy reveals that was indeed the cause of death. Which would seem a logical assumption at this stage of things. There were no signs of struggle?"

"None that I could see. Uh, in Melanie's apartment, you might say there were always signs of struggle. I mean, she wasn't the world's most fanatical housekeeper."

"But nothing out of the ordinary? And no sign of another person's presence?"

"No. Except the phone off the hook, of course. I hung up myself after I called the police."

"And neglected to mention to the police that it had been off the hook when you arrived?"

"I felt they would wonder why I happened to notice it."

He nodded. "And they'd resent you for it. It's infinitely

31

simpler for them to process this as an accidental overdose than as a murder, and a loose end like a telephone off the hook would only impress them as a complication. They'd file the case the same way, but they would be annoyed with you for bringing up irrelevancies and inconsistencies. They would have been happiest if you could have told them Melanie had been planning on trying heroin. It's as well you didn't, but that's how any bureaucratic mind works."

He spun around in his swivel chair and gazed into the fishtank at eye level. The entire room, and it is a large one, is paneled in English oak and lined from floor to ceiling with shelves. Most of the shelf space is devoted to books, the overwhelming majority of them detective stories, but fish tanks are spotted here and there on the shelves. There are a dozen of them. They are all what Haig calls recreational aquariums, as opposed to the breeding tanks and rearing tanks on the top floor. Actually, to tell you the truth, they're what Haig calls recreational *aquaria*. I call them aquariums because I'm not entirely literate yet.

This particular tank was very restful to look at. It was a fifteen-gallon tank, which means it was one foot deep by one foot wide by two feet long, and its sole occupants were eleven *Rasbora heteramorpha*. I have a feeling that you either know what they are or you don't, and a description won't help much, but Haig wants me to make an effort on matters like this. Rasboras are fish about an inch long, a delicate rose pink with a blackish wedge on their sides. They're pretty, and they swim in schools, and in this particular tank they swam in and around a dwarf amazon sword plant and a piece of crystalline quartz. The tank was top-lighted, and if you watched the fish for a while you got a happy feeling.

At least I did. Haig watched the fish for a while and stroked his beard a lot and turned around in the swivel chair with a thoughtful expression on his face.

"How old was Melanie?"

"I don't know. A little older than me. I guess about twenty-one."

"And Jessica?"

"Older, but I don't know by how much. Wait a minute. Melanie was the second youngest. And Robin was older than she was, so one of the girls still alive is younger than Melanie."

"Were any of them married?"

"Yes, but I don't know which ones. Obviously Melanie wasn't married." And never would be, I thought, and something vaguely resembling a lump formed in my throat, but I swallowed and it went away.

Haig said, "Hmmmmmm." He turned and looked at the rasboras some more. I watched him do this for a while and saw that it was going to be an extensive thing, so I got up and went over to the wall and looked at some fish myself. A pair of African gouramis, two very beautiful fish, rendered in shades of chocolate. I'm not putting down the Latin name, because there's no agreement on it yet; the species was just discovered a couple of years ago and has never been bred in captivity, a state of affairs which Leo Haig regards as a personal challenge. I stared into the tank and decided that I had never seen two living creatures display less interest in each other. We will breed the damned things sooner or later, but we were not going to accomplish it that particular evening.

Nor were we going to accomplish much else. Haig swung around and said as much. "*Sitzfleisch*," was how he put it. "We have to let the newspapers do some of our work for us, and then you can go to the public library and do some of the rest. At the moment the library is closed and the newspaper has not yet materialized, so we exercise our sitting flesh. Get the chessboard."

I got the chessboard. I didn't much want to get the chessboard, but I could see no way out of it. Leo Haig was about as effective at chess as he was at smoking a pipe. Whenever there was nothing to do he was apt to want to play. I'm not very good myself. When I worked in the whorehouse in South Carolina, most of my job consisted of playing chess with Geraldine. She almost always beat me, and I in turn almost always beat Leo Haig.

We played three quick games, and they went as they usually did. I exchanged a knight for a rook in the first game and wore him down, and in the second I put a strong queen-side attack together and more or less lucked into a mating combination. In the last game he left his queen *en prise*, and when I pointed it out to him he tipped his king over and resigned gracefully.

"I've a feeling," he said, "that I shall never be a satisfactory chess player."

I didn't want to argue and knew better than to agree.

"I don't think the character tag of being a hopeless chess player will endear me to the reading public," he continued.

I still didn't say anything.

"We shall pursue this a bit further," he went on. "But I think we must ultimately find another sport. In your spare moments, Chip, you might compile a list of sedentary sports requiring a certain degree of mental dexterity."

We had coffee together, and then he went upstairs to discuss chess openings with the upstairs fish. I wandered into the front room and played a quick game of backgammon with Wong. He said, "Ah, so," a lot, which I think is why Haig hired him, and he beat the hell out of me. Then I went downstairs and around the corner for a beer.

Leo Haig's house is on West 20th Street between Eighth and Ninth Avenues, which puts it just two blocks away from my rooming house. (Which is why I selected the rooming house in the first place; before I went to work for Haig I was living on the Upper West Side, near Columbia Unviersity.) I promised I would tell you about Haig's house, and I guess now is as good a time as any.

The address is 311½ West 20th, and the ½ is because it does not front on the street. There's a house out in front, and there's an alley next to it, and if you buzz the buzzer a door opens and you can walk down the alley to the house in back, which is half Leo Haig's and half a whorehouse. It started off life as a carriage house. Many years ago, rich people lived in the house on the street and had the one in back for their horses and servants. The horses lived on the bottom and the servants on top. Now the horses have been replaced by Puerto Rican prostitutes and the servants have been replaced by Leo Haig and Wong Fat.

My rooming house is a compromise. Haig wants me to live

in the carriage house. There's an extra room on the lower floor that's at least as spacious as the one I pay twenty dollars a week for, two blocks to the south. It's furnished nicely and it's reassuringly devoid of cockroaches, which are fairly abundant in my place on 18th Street. He keeps trying to move me in there and I keep resisting.

"The thing is," I told him finally, "I'm sort of, uh, interested in girls. I mean, sometimes something comes along that looks like the foundation of a meaningful relationship, uh, and, uh—"

Haig's pipe stiffened, which doesn't happen often. "Your friends would always be welcome in my house," he said.

"It's not that, exactly."

"Your relations with women are your own business. It's been my observation that the great detectives are inclined to be celibate. Not through inadequacy, but because they have passed through the stage of sexual activity before developing their highest powers. Wolfe, of course, fathered a daughter before embracing misogyny wholeheartedly. Holmes was devoted to The Woman but lived alone. Perry Mason never so much as took hold of Della Street's hand. Poirot always had an eye for a pretty figure, but no more than his eye was ever engaged. Their assistants, however, were apt to go to the opposite extreme. I don't want to put too fine a point on this, but I would have no objection to your leading an active sexual life. You could bring women here, Chip. They could attend the breakfast table with no embarrassment."

But of course the embarrassment would come long before they got to the breakfast table. Because you cannot make an initial pitch to a girl and lead her up an alleyway and into what is unmistakably a Puerto Rican whorehouse without creating an atmosphere which is not precisely perfect. So I keep my room on 18th Street, and consistently fail to lure girls to it anyway, and Haig and I maintain this running argument.

I drank two beers at Dominick's and hung around there until the late news came and went. There was nothing about Melanie, which wasn't all that surprising. If every drug overdose made the eleven o'clock news, they wouldn't have

35

time for wars or assassinations. I threw darts at Dominick's dart board without distinguishing myself. I thought a lot about Melanie, and I remembered what she'd been like alive and how she had looked in death, and all of a sudden I was very damned glad I was working for Leo Haig, because we were going to get the son of a bitch who killed her and nail his hide to the wall.

4

IN THE MORNING THE MAN NEXT door had a coughing fit, and I woke up before the alarm clock went off. I picked up a *Times* on the way over to Haig's house. In the courtyard, Carmelita was hanging out underwear on a clothesline running between two ailanthus trees. I have a lot of respect for those trees; anything that can come up out of a crack in a New York sidewalk deserves a lot of credit.

"You up early," she said.

"So are you."

"I am not go to bed yet. Busy night."

"Business is good, huh?"

"All time sailors. Want to fock like crazy. Drink and fock, drink and fock."

"Well," I said.

"Margarita, she so sore. Fockin' sailors. Mos' tricks, all they want is the blow job. Get the other from their wife. Fockin' sailors, they get blow job alla time on the boat, alla they wanna do is fock. So everybody gets sore."

"Oh," I said.

I went upstairs and into the office. Haig was busy playing with his fish tanks. I opened the paper and found the article about Melanie and started reading it. Wong came in on tiptoe with a couple of cups of strong coffee. He and I smiled at each other and he went away. Haig went on feeding the fish and I went on reading. A couple of paragraphs from the bottom I must have voiced a thought without realizing it, because Haig turned to face me and said, "Why?"

"Huh?"

"You said you'll be a son of a bitch. I was wondering why."

"I knew she had some income," I said. "But I never thought it amounted to that much. I mean, she never even offered to

37

pay for her own brown rice, for Pete's sake."

"Make sense, Chip."

I blinked at him. "I was right about her age," I said. "She turned twenty-one in May and came into the principal of her inheritance. According to the *Times* her share came to a little over two million dollars."

"Interesting," he said.

"But then why did she live like that? Suppose she didn't want to touch the principal, what would the interest be on two million dollars?"

"Well over a hundred thousand dollars a year."

"I'll be a son of a bitch."

"So you've said."

"I used to buy subway tokens for her. She could have gone home in a limousine. It's unreal."

He seated himself on his side of the desk and held out his hand for the paper. I gave it to him and he read the article through several times, pausing to stroke his beard between paragraphs. Now and then he made a sort of clicking sound with his tongue or teeth. I don't know how he makes that sound exactly or just what it's supposed to indicate. When he had read most of the print off the page he set the paper down and closed his eyes for a moment.

Then he said, "You have your notebook? Good. There are several things you have to do. The funeral is at two tomorrow afternoon. Had you planned to go?"

"I hadn't even thought about it. Of course I'll go."

"I think you should, for reasons in addition to your feelings for Miss Trelawney. In the meantime, there are places you should go and people you might profitably meet."

He talked for a while, and I wrote things down in my notebook.

I got to the library at 42nd and Fifth a little before the lunch crowd took over the steps. I went through the *New York Times Index* for the past three years and made a lot of notes, then headed over to the microfilm room and filled out a request slip. A girl with Dick Tracy's chin brought me little boxes of film and showed me how to use the viewer.

At first it was slow going because I tended to get sidetracked. I would be scanning my way through back issues and happen to hit an article that looked interesting, so I would stop and read it. After this happened a couple of times I realized what was going on and kept my mind on what I was there for.

Cyrus Trelawney had died three years ago. A combination of heart trouble, cirrhosis of the liver and general cussedness had taken him out five days after his eighty-first birthday. He was a widower at the time, and he left five daughters. The eldest, Caitlin, was then thirty-three. The others were Robin (twenty-seven), Jessica (twenty-one), Melanie (eighteen) and Kim (fifteen). It seemed to me that there ought to have been a thirty-year-old between Caitlin and Robin, just to preserve the symmetry. Maybe he'd had financial reverses around that time.

Although he didn't seem to have had many financial reverses generally. The *Times* obit must have been an easy one to write, because Trelawney seems to have been a properly crusty old pirate. He had come to the States from Cornwall at the age of sixteen with a couple of silver shillings in his shoe, and I guess he was better at finding A Job With A Future than I'll ever be, because in the next sixty-five years he parlayed those shillings into almost eleven million dollars, after taxes. He did most of this in ways that I'm not equipped to understand, financial transactions and mergers and takeovers and all those words you find in the business pages of the newspaper.

Trelawney used to claim he was descended from Cornish pirates, and the *Times* writer sort of implied that no one had any reason to doubt his claim on the basis of his performance in the world of finance. He was past forty before he married, and shortly thereafter he set about producing daughters at three-year intervals, except for the one gap of six years. He was twenty years older than his wife and he outlived her by eight years.

I got a lot of information from the obituary notice and more information from various social page articles and the stories about the deaths of Robin and Jessica, but there's no particular point in saying just what I learned where. I had to report it that way to Leo Haig, but I'll just sketch in the general facts here.

Caitlin, the firstborn, was thirty-six now. She had been married at sixteen, but old Cyrus had it annulled. She was married again six years later, divorced two years after that, married again the following year and divorced again within a year. Now she was married for the fourth time — unless there had been a divorce since then that hadn't made the papers. A couple of months before her father's death, she'd exchanged gold bands with Gregory Depew Vandiver, of the Sands Point Vandivers, whoever the hell they are. The wedding announcement told all the schools he had attended and all the clubs he belonged to and described him as connected with a Wall Street firm with half a dozen very Protestant names in its title. After a honeymoon in Gstaad, *The Times* said, the Vandivers would make their home on the North Shore of Long Island.

Robin had been married twice. When she was twenty-three she married Phillip Flanner, a man twice her age who had been her psych professor at Sarah Lawrence. Two years after the wedding, Flanner fell in front of a subway train. If your wife's that rich, what are you doing in the subway? Robin remarried three years after that. Her second husband was Ferdinand Bell. (I kept writing this down as Ferdinand Bull, by the way.) The article described Bell as a professional numismatist, which is what a coin dealer becomes when he marries an heiress.

Robin's auto wreck — Haig said not to call it an accident — took place in Cobleskill, New York, in January. She and her husband were returning from a three-day convention of the Empire State Numismatic Association held in Utica. There was a patch of ice on the road and Bell lost control of the car. He was wearing his seat belt and sustained superficial injuries. Robin was in back taking a nap and was not wearing a seatbelt. She broke her neck, among quite a few other things, and died instantly.

Jessica went out the window three months after Robin's death. The window she went out of was in the penthouse of the Correggio, one of the more desirable high-rise apartment buildings in the Village. She had lived in the penthouse with a girl named Andrea Sugar, who had been working at the time of the fall at Indulgence, which was described as an East Side massage parlor and recreation center. Jessica also worked at Indulgence as a recreational therapist, but had taken the afternoon off.

Jessica had never been married, and by reading between the lines I developed a fair idea why.

Melanie you know about.

I couldn't learn very much about Kim. She had been only fifteen when her father died and was only eighteen now. I could tell you what high school she attended but I don't think you'd care any more than I did. The items I turned up through the *Times Index* were not much help by the time I found them on microfilm. They just mentioned her as "also appearing" in a variety of off-off-Broadway shows. The shows in which she also appeared got uniformly rotten reviews. In one review, a brief pan of something called *America, You Suck!* the critic wrote: "Young Kim Trelawney constitutes the one bright spot in this otherwise unmitigated disaster. Although not called upon to act, Miss Trelawney is unquestionably an ornament to the stage."

By the time I left the library I had sore eyes from the viewer and a sore right hand from scribbling in my notebook. I also had the name of the lawyer who had handled Cyrus Trelawney's affairs. I called him from a phone booth and learned that he was out to lunch, which reminded me that I ought to be out to lunch myself. I went to the Alamo and had a plate of chili with beans. They charge an extra fifteen cents for any dish without beans. Don't ask me why.

The pay phone at the Alamo was out of order. So were the first two booths I tried, and before I found a third one I decided not to call him anyway. It wasn't likely he'd be desperately anxious to see me, and it's always easier to get rid of a pest over the phone than in person.

His name was Addison Shivers, and if I was making this up I wouldn't dream of fastening a name like that onto him, because it didn't fit him at all. I expected someone tall and cadaverous and permanently constipated. I can't tell you anything about the state of his bowels, actually, but he was nothing like what I had anticipated. To begin with, it wasn't hard to get to see him at all.

His office was on Chambers Street, near City Hall. I took the subway there and found the building and was elevated to the sixth floor, where a frosted glass window said *Addison Shivers/ Attorney-at-Law*. Then there were half a dozen other names in much smaller print underneath. I don't happen to remember a single one of them.

I told the witch at the desk that my name was Harrison and I worked for Leo Haig. (If you give that the right inflection, people think they've heard of Haig even though they haven't.) I said I wanted to see Mr. Shivers. She went through a door and came back to ask what my visit was in reference to.

"Melanie Trelawney," I said. She relayed this and came back with the news that Mr. Shivers would see me. She seemed even more surprised than I was.

His office was very simple, very sparsely furnished. I guess you have to be richer than God to have the confidence to get away with that. All the furniture was oak, and you could tell right away that he hadn't bought it in an antique shop; he had bought it brand-new and kept it for fifty years. The only decorative things were a couple of sailing prints in inexpensive frames and some brass fixtures from ships. I think one of them was what is called a sextant, but I honestly don't know enough about that sort of thing to tell you what the rest of them were. Or even to swear that the one was a sextant, for that matter.

He looked old enough to be Cyrus Trelawney's father. He had a little white hair left around the rim of his head. His face was sort of red, and his nose was more than sort of red. He was well padded, although you couldn't call him fat. The strongest impression I got from him was one of genuine benevolence. He just plain looked like a nice man. Sometimes you can't tell, but then again, sometimes you can.

"You'll excuse me if I don't stand," he said. His voice was dry but gentle. "I read about Melanie, of course. When that sort of thing happens I merely wish they could hold off until I either die or become senile. I've given up asking that tragedy be averted entirely. I merely wish to be spared the knowledge of it." He looked off into space for a moment, then returned his eyes to mine. "I didn't see Melanie often after her father's death. But I always liked her. She was a good person."

"Yes, she was."

"Your name is Harrison, I believe. And you work for a man named Haig, but I don't believe I know him."

"Leo Haig," I said. "The detective."

"No, I don't know him. I don't know any detectives, I don't believe. Any living detectives. What's your connection with Melanie Trelawney?"

I'd had a whole approach planned, but it didn't seem to fit the person Addison Shivers turned out to be. "It's not much of a connection," I said. "I knew her for the past month; she was my friend."

"And?"

"She was murdered," I said. "Leo Haig and I are trying to find out who killed her."

This, let me tell you, was not part of the original game plan. Haig had emphasized that there was no need to pass on our suspicions and convictions to anyone else for the time being. But he had also always told me about instinct guided by experience, or intuition guided by experience, or intelligence guided by experience, and that's what I was using.

Mr. Shivers sat there and listened while I told him all the reasons why Leo Haig and I knew Melanie had been murdered. He knew how to listen, and his eyes showed that he was following what he was hearing. He heard me all the way through and then asked a few questions, such as why I had not mentioned any of this to the police, and when I answered his questions he nodded and sat forward in his chair and folded his hands on the top of his old oak desk.

After a moment he said, "You'll want information, of course. About the will, about the disposition of funds. I can tell you all that." He got a remote look in his eyes again. "Poor Cyrus," he said. "He was my client for fifty years, you know. Needless to say he employed a great many other attorneys, but I was his lawyer in all personal matters. And he was my friend for as long as he was my client. He was a very great man, you know."

"He must have been."

"A great man. I'm not sure that he was a *good* man, mind you. Goodness and greatness rarely keep house together. But I can say that he was a good friend. And now three of his daughters are dead. And his only son."

"His son?"

"Cyrus, Junior. He was the second born, he died in infancy. Cyrus never ceased to mourn him, especially when it became evident that he would not be fathering any more children. He wanted the name continued, you see. He was resigned to the fact that it would not be, ultimately, and felt it would be sufficient that his seed would endure through his daughters." He cleared his throat. "And now three of his daughters are dead in less than a year."

Cyrus, Jr. That explained the six-year gap between Caitlin and Robin.

"I respect your logic concerning Melanie's death," he said. "I agree that she must almost certainly have been murdered. You realize, of course, that this does not call for the conclusion that Robin and Jessica were murdered as well."

"I know."

"Though one cannot deny the possibility. Or the danger to the two remaining Trelawney girls."

I nodded.

"What do you and Mr. Haig intend to do?"

"Try to warn Mrs. Vandiver and Kim. And try to figure out who killed Melanie and how to prove it."

"You ought to have a client," he said. He opened his desk drawer and took out a large checkbook, the kind with three checks on a page. He wrote out a check, noted it on the stub, and handed it across the desk to me. It was made out to Leo Haig and the amount was a thousand dollars.

"I don't know what your rates are," he said. Neither, to tell you the truth, did I. "This will serve as a retainer. Note that I am engaging you to look out for the interests of Cyrus

44

Trelawney, deceased. That leaves you a considerable degree of leeway."

"I think I understand."

He had one of his junior clerks find various papers about the Trelawney estate. He went over them with me and explained the parts I couldn't understand, and I filled the rest of my notebook. He poured himself a large brandy in the course of this, and asked me if I wanted anything myself. I told him I didn't.

When I had everything he could give me, he excused himself again for not getting to his feet. He leaned across the desk and we shook hands.

I asked if I would be seeing him the following day at Melanie's funeral.

"No, I don't go to funerals any more," he said. "If I did, I shouldn't have time for anything else."

5

I HAD NEVER BEEN TO A FUNERAL BEFORE. When my parents committed suicide, I was away at school. I suppose the funeral took place before I could have gotten to it, but I have to admit I never even thought about it. I just packed a bag and started hitchhiking.

If Melanie's funeral was typical, I'm surprised the custom hasn't died out. I mean, I can sort of understand the way the Irish do it. Everybody stays drunk for three or four days. That makes a certain amount of sense. But here we were all gathered in this stark, modernistic, non-denominational cesspool on Lexington and 54th in the middle of the afternoon, listening to a man who had never met her say dumb things about a dead girl. One of the worst parts was that the jerk was sort of glossing over the fact that Melanie was either a junkie or a suicide, or both. He didn't come right out and say anything about casting first stones, but you could see it was running through his mind. I wanted to jump up and tell the world Melanie was murdered. I managed to control myself.

I wouldn't have been telling the world, anyway. Just a tiny portion of it. There were none of Melanie's friends there except me. Her relationships with the people in her neighborhood had been deliberately casual, and even if some of them had decided to come to the funeral, they would have been too stoned to get it all together. *"Hey, man, like we got to go see them plant old Melanie." "No, baby, that was last week." "Far out!"*

I recognized Caitlin and Kim with no trouble. I would have figured out who they were anyway since they were seated in the front pew, but the family resemblance was unmistakable. They didn't exactly look alike, and they didn't look like Melanie exactly, but all of them looked like old Cyrus Trelawney. Except on them it looked becoming. They had what I guess we

46

can call the Trelawney nose, strong and assertive, and the deep-set eyes. Caitlin was blond and fair-skinned, a tall woman, expensively dressed. The man beside her wore a tweed suit that didn't have leather elbow patches yet. His nose and lips were thin and his expression was pained. I didn't have much trouble figuring out that he was Gregory Vandiver. Of the Sands Point Vandivers.

Kim was very short and slender, also fair-skinned, but with hair as dark as Melanie's. She seemed to be crying a lot, which set her apart from the rest of the company. Crying or not, I could see what the theater critic meant; she would have been an ornament to any stage. The guy next to her, on the other hand, had no decorative effect whatsoever. He kept reaching over and patting her hand. He looked familiar, and I finally figured out where I had seen him before. He played the title role in *King Kong*.

Kim was wearing a simple black dress, and she managed simultaneously to look good in it and to give the impression that she didn't generally wear dresses. The ape was wearing a suit for the first time in his life.

There was a handful of other people I hadn't seen before and couldn't identify. I guessed that the plump, boyish man in the gray sharkskin suit might be Ferdinand Bell, Robin's husband. If there was a professional numismatist in the room, he was likely to be it. And a girl off to one side was probably Andrea Sugar, if Andrea Sugar was there at all, because nobody else around could possibly have been a recreational therapist at something called Indulgence. The rest of the crowd was mostly old, and you sensed somehow that they were there because they liked funerals better than daytime television. I understand there are a lot of people like that. Every couple of days they trot down to the local mortuary to see who's playing.

The casket was open. I guess they do this so that the more skeptical mourners can assure themselves that the person they're mourning is genuinely dead. And so that the undertaker can show off his cosmetic skill.

I wasn't going to look. But then I decided that was silly, and I went up and looked, and it wasn't Melanie at all. There was rouge on her cheeks and lipstick on her mouth and eyebrow pencil on her eyebrows and some tasteless shit had cut her pretty hair and styled it, if you could call it that. Melanie never wore makeup in her life. This wasn't Melanie. This was a reject from the waxworks.

I really felt like hitting somebody.

Haig had told me to approach one of the sisters after the funeral. It was up to me which one I chose. "The older girl is probably better equipped to make a decision," he said, "while the younger one would probably be more receptive to overtures from someone your age. Use your judgment."

I used my judgment, and decided Kim might well be more receptive to overtures from someone my age, especially in view of the fact that I was more receptive to the idea of making them to her than to Caitlin. But I used a little more of my judgment and came to the conclusion that I would rather talk to Kim without that Neanderthal of hers hulking nearby. The idea of trying to Broach A Serious Subject to her while she was intermittently dissolving in tears also left something to be desired. So it was Caitlin by default.

If you don't mind, I won't go into detail about the trip to the cemetery or the burial. I rode out in a car full of old ladies talking about convertible debentures. There was a machine at the graveside to lower the casket, untouched by human hands, and off in the distance a couple of old men stood leaning on their shovels. They reminded me of the vultures in cartoons about people lost in the desert.

Anyway, the same limousines drove everybody back from Long Island and deposited us in front of the mortuary, and I managed to walk over to Caitlin Vandiver and her husband. I introduced myself and asked if I could talk with her about Melanie.

I got a smile from her and a blank look from him, and I also got the impression that she smiled a lot and he looked blank a lot. "So you were a friend of Melanie's," she said. "Well, I don't know that I can tell you very much about her. I don't even know what you would want to hear. We were never terribly

48

close, you know. I'm several years older than she was."

She paused there, as if waiting for me to express doubt. She didn't look old by any means. I'm a terrible judge of age, but I probably would have guessed her at thirty and I knew she was six years older than that.

"There are a couple of things," I said. "I think it would be worthwhile for us to talk."

Her smile froze up a little, and at the same time her eyes showed a little more than the polite interest they had held earlier. "I see," she said.

I don't know what she saw.

"Well," she said, the smile in full force again, "actually I could use some company. I hate to eat alone and funerals always make me ravenous. Is that shameful, do you think?"

I mumbled some dumb thing or other. Caitlin turned to her husband and put her cheek out for a kiss. He picked up his cue and kissed her.

"Greg always plays squash on Fridays," she said. "Neither rain nor snow nor heat nor gloom of night, you understand." The two of them said pleasant things to one another and Vandiver strode athletically down the street, arms swinging at his sides. I decided that he probably jogged every morning.

"He jogs every morning before breakfast," Caitlin said. It unsettles me when people do this. I feel as though I must have a window in the middle of my forehead. "He's keeping himself in marvellous physical condition."

"That's very good," I said.

"Oh, it's simply great. I wonder what he thinks he's saving himself for. I haven't had a really decent orgasm with him since the first time I saw him in his jogging suit. Romance tiptoed out the window. Shall we eat? I know a charming little French place near here. Never crowded, quite intimate, and they make a decent Martini; and if I don't have one soon — fellow me lad — I shall positively *die*."

And, after we had walked about a block, she said, "I pick the wrong words sometimes, damn it. I shouldn't have said that about positively dying. Too many people are doing it lately. Robin, Jessica, now Melanie. It's scary, isn't it?"

She took my hand as she said this and gave it a squeeze. I gave a squeeze back, and I think she smiled when I did.

We went to a restaurant on 48th Street. It was empty, except for a couple of serious drinkers at the bar and a couple at a side table trying to stretch out lunch so that it reached all the way to quitting time. We walked through to the garden in the rear and took a table.

"Tanqueray Martini, straight up, bone dry, twist," she told the waiter. It sounded as though she'd had practice with the line. To me she said, "Do you drink? I know so many people your age don't these days."

I'd been trying to decide between a Coke and a beer, but that did it. "Double Irish whiskey," I said. "With water back."

Her eyebrows went up, but just a little. She told me I was to call her Caitlin. I was not certain that I was going to do this, and supposed I would sidestep the issue by not calling her anything at all. She seemed to think Harrison was my first name and wanted to know what my last name was, and I told her, and she got a little rattled and said that Harrison Harrison was unusual, to say the least, and ultimately we got that straightened out. She didn't ask me what Chip was short for, which was one strong point in her favor.

There were other points in her favor. Maybe her husband jogged every morning before breakfast because he was trying to catch up with her. The money she spent on her clothes and her hair didn't hurt, but it didn't account for her figure or the general youthfulness of her appearance. She was tall for a woman, and quite slender, and her breasts were not especially easy to ignore.

There was more to it than all that, though. She was damned attractive and damned well knew it, and she knew how to play off this attractiveness and, oh, hell, there's only one way to say it. She was very good at getting people horny.

She ordered mussels and a glass of wine and another Martini. I didn't want anything to eat, which surprised her but didn't seem to annoy her. She made a lot of small talk during her meal, and when I would start to turn the conversation around to Melanie she managed to sidetrack it. After this happened a few

50

times I stopped thinking that she was more shook up than she was showing and Got The Message.

What I remembered, actually, was one time when I was taken out to lunch by Joe Elder, who is my editor. We went to a place around the corner from his office where they have a working antique telephone on each table. The food is better than you'd expect. The only thing wrong with Mr. Elder is that he can actually drink a Daiquiri without making a face. God knows how. But all through lunch I kept trying to talk about an idea I had for a book, and he kept changing the subject, and later they brought the coffee and he started talking about the book, and it was the same way now with Caitlin Vandiver. She had decided that we were having a business lunch and she knew that meant not saying a word about business until we were done with the lunch.

She finished her mussels about the same time I ran out of Irish to sip at. When the coffee came she settled herself in her chair and came in right on cue.

"You were a friend of Melanie's," she said.

Which was my cue, so I picked it up. "I was the one who discovered the body," I said.

"Oh dear. That must have been awful for you."

It had been, but that wasn't what I wanted to talk about. I told her I was concerned professionally, which brought that tension into her expression, which I later realized was because she thought I might be working up to some sort of blackmail pitch. But I went on to say that I worked for Leo Haig. "The prominent detective," I said.

"Oh, yes."

Sure, lady. "I have to tell you this in confidence. We have grounds to believe that Melanie was murdered."

"But I thought it was an overdose of heroin."

"It was." The autopsy had confirmed this. "That doesn't mean she gave it to herself."

"I see." She thought for a minute. Then she said, "Oh."

"I'm afraid so. It puts things in sort of a different light. Jessica's suicide and Robin's accident—"

"Might not be a suicide and an accident. Well, Robin's

51

certainly was, although I suppose someone could have tampered with Ferdie's car. Do those things happen? I know they do in books, but my God, if I were going to kill someone I would take my trusty little gun and shoot him in the back of the head." She was silent for a moment, and I wondered who she was killing in fantasy. (Whom, I mean.) Then she said, "I never thought Jessica was the type to commit suicide. She was always a tougher and bitchier broad than I am, and that's going some. And she was a dyke, too."

I had sort of assumed this, but I still didn't have a reply worked out.

"Of course she might have grown out of that," Caitlin went on. "I did, you know. Although I never embraced lesbianism as wholeheartedly as Jessica did. I never stopped liking men, you see."

"Uh," I said.

"Do you want to know something interesting? When I was a girl, oh, way back before Noah built his ark, I always had a special preference for older men."

"Er."

"But now that I've slithered onto the dark side of thirty, I find I've done an about-face. I have a thing for young men these days."

"Uh."

"I've noticed, Chip, that some young men have a thing for older women."

I don't have a thing for older women, but I certainly haven't got anything against them. Actually, I don't suppose chronological age means very much. There are women of thirty-six who are too old. There are other women the same age who are not. Caitlin was in the second category, and I was becoming more aware of this every minute.

Her perfume may have had something to do with this. Her leg, which had somehow moved against mine under the table, may also have had something to do with it.

"Well," I said. "About Melanie—"

"Were you sleeping with her, Chip?"

Everybody wanted to know if I was sleeping with Melanie.

52

First those cops, now Caitlin. I said, "We hadn't known each other very long."

"Sometimes it doesn't take very long."

"Er. The thing is, you know, that someone killed Melanie. And if someone also killed Jessica, and if it's the same someone—"

"Then Kim and I might be on somebody's Christmas list."

"Uh-huh. Something like that."

She lit a cigarette. She had been lighting cigarettes all along, but I don't think it's absolutely essential to call it to your attention every time somebody lights a cigarette. This time, though, she made a production number out of it, winding up taking a big drag and sighing out a cloud of smoke.

She said, "You know, Chip, I do have a little trouble taking this seriously."

"There may not be anything to it."

"But there also *may* be something to it, is that what you mean? Assuming there is, what do I do about it? Put myself in a convent? Hire around-the-clock bodyguards? Quickly marry the president so I qualify for Secret Service protection?"

"The most important thing is to find Melanie's killer."

" 'Catch him before he kills more?' That makes a certain amount of sense." She studied me for a moment. "The man you work for," she said.

"Leo Haig."

"He's really good?"

"He's brilliant."

"Hmmm. And what do you do for him exactly? You're a little young to be a detective, aren't you?"

"I'm his assistant. That doesn't mean my job is taking out the garbage." Actually, I do take the garbage out of the fish tanks some of the time. "I work with him on cases."

"So you'd be working on this, too."

"That's right. I do the leg work." I regretted saying that because she sort of winked and did some leg work of her own.

"I'll just bet you do, Chip."

"Uh."

"I'd like to see you devote all your energies to my case," she

53

said. As I guess you've noticed, she tended to say things with double meanings. "I'd like you working hard on my behalf. You don't have a client, do you? You're just investigating because of your friendship for my sister?"

We had a client but he didn't want his name mentioned, so I didn't mention it. I agreed that we were involved in this out of friendship for Melanie. Which was true — I would have been working every bit as hard without Addison Shivers as a client.

She opened her bag and found a checkbook. She wrote for a minute, tore out a check, folded it in half and slipped it to me. "That's an advance," she said.

I took the check.

"An advance," she repeated. "Actually this is no day to be making advances, is it?"

"Uh."

"It's about that time, isn't it? I have to pick up my darling husband at his club. On the way home I can hear how good it is to work up a sweat. That depends how you work it up, don't you think?"

"I guess."

"Do you? I suspect you do. I have that feeling about you, Chip. And I'm sure we'll see a lot of each other in the course of your investigation of the case."

"I'm sure we will, Mrs Vandiver."

"Caitlin."

"Caitlìn," I agreed.

"It's a difficult name to remember, isn't it?"

"No, but—"

"Some of my best friends call me Cat. Just plain Cat. You know, as in pussy."

The waiter brought the check. She put money on the table and we left. I was really in no condition to walk, to tell you the truth, and I think she noticed this, and I think she was pleased.

On the street she offered me her cheek as she had offered it to her husband, but when I went to kiss her, she turned her head quickly and my mouth landed on hers. She did something very nice with her tongue, then drew quickly away, an amused light in her eyes.

54

"Oh, we'll get along," she said.

I felt like springing for a cab, so of course there weren't any around. I took the subway. It was hot and crowded and smelly and I wound up pressed up against a home-bound secretary. I was in the wrong condition to be pressed up against anyone and the secretary noticed it. She gave me the look people give when they find a cockroach in their oatmeal.

When I got off the train I finally looked at Caitlin's check. It was for five hundred dollars and it was made out to me rather than to Haig. She'd spelled my first name Chipp, which explained why she hadn't asked me what my real name was. She was probably used to people with first names like that.

Actually, it would simplify my life in a lot of ways if I spelled it with two p's. I should have thought of that years ago.

Haig didn't see anything wrong with accepting retainers from both Addison Shivers and Caitlin Vandiver. "Our work will be in both their interests," he said. "I see no likely conflict. And there's certainly precedent for it. Nero Wolfe frequently represents more than one person in the same matter, and does so without either party being aware of his association with the other. In the case that was reported under the title *Too Many Clients*, for example—"

I had just read *Too Many Clients* a month or so ago, but there was no point in telling him that. You might as well try telling Billy Graham you read the Bible once, for all the good it would do you.

6

I WAS UPSTAIRS UNTIL SIX-THIRTY, helping Haig with the fish. He had a strain of sailfin mollies he was trying to fix. The object was to develop the dorsal fin to the greatest possible size through selective breeding and inbreeding and by giving the young the best possible nutritional start on life. One of the molly mothers had dropped young earlier in the day and we had to net her and remove her from the breeding tank. Mollies are less likely to eat their young than most livebearers, but every once in a while you get a female who hasn't read the book, and she can polish off an entire generation in a couple of hungry hours.

We gave the babies a heavy feeding of live brine shrimp. Haig buys enormous quantities of frozen brine shrimp for general use, but hatches his own for feeding young fishes. He tends to be a fanatic about things like this, and while he fed live brine shrimp to a few dozen tanks of young fish, I hosed out one of the tubs and prepared a brine mixture and sprinkled the little dry eggs on it.

Then we went downstairs and Wong announced that dinner was ready, and it was a Szechuan shrimp dish with scallions and those little black peppers that it is a terrible idea to bite into. Wong's shrimps had very little in common with the ones I had been feeding to our fish. He's a fairly sensational cook, and never seems to make the same thing twice.

I stayed around long enough to win a few games of chess. Then I went downstairs and said polite things to Consuela and Carmelita and Maria and some other girls whose names I didn't know, and let Juana the Madame pinch my cheek, which I wish she would stop doing, and then I started walking downtown.

The Cornelia Street Theater was located in a basement. You

can probably guess what street it was on. There was a banner outside at street level announcing that they were doing *Uncle Vanya*, by Chekhov.

Maybe you know what the play is about. If not, I'm not going to be much help to you. I paid two dollars for a ticket and sat fairly close to the stage. (Actually, there were only about fifty seats in the house, so it wouldn't have been possible to sit very far from the stage.) Maybe thirty of the fifty seats were empty. I sat and watched the play without paying any attention to it. I don't know whether it was good or not. I just couldn't concentrate. I would drift off into thought chains and just let my mind wander all over the place, and once in a while Kim Trelawney would appear on stage and I would take some time out to look at her, but she didn't have many lines and never hung around long, and as soon as she went off I went off myself.

I guess the show must go on, although with this show I couldn't quite see it. I mean, anybody could have played Kim's part that night, for all she had to do up there. And it wasn't as though an audience of thousands would have killed themselves if they didn't see *Uncle Vanya* that night. The way she had acted at the funeral, obviously taking it all hard, I hadn't really expected her to show up for the play.

There were two intermissions, and each of them drained a little of the audience away, so by the time the final curtain went down there were only about a dozen of us there to applaud, and not all of us did it very enthusiastically. The cast tried to take two bows, but by the time the curtain came up a second time everybody had already stopped applauding and people were on their way out of the theater. It was sort of sad.

I managed to get backstage and meet Kim. She blinked a little while I introduced myself, and when I said I was a friend of Melanie's, she nodded in recognition. "I saw you at the funeral," she said.

"I'd like to talk to you, if I could."

"About Melanie?"

"Sort of."

"I'll meet you out front," she said. "Just give me a few minutes."

She took about four of them, and came out wearing jeans and a peasant blouse and carrying a canvas shoulder bag in red, white and blue. She suggested we have coffee at O'John's, a little place on the corner of West 4th.

"Gordie's going to meet me there in a few minutes," she said. "He doesn't like me walking home alone."

We got a window table and ordered two cups of coffee. "Gordie's a little overprotective," she said. "Sometimes it bothers me. But sometimes I like it."

"Was Gordie the fellow you were with this afternoon?"

"Yes." She smiled suddenly, and instantly reminded me very much of Melanie, the way her entire face was so immediately transformed by her smile. "I haven't known him very long," she said, "and I don't really know him very well. In certain ways, that is. He's very different from the type of boy I usually go out with."

"How?"

"Well, you know. He's not educated; he dropped out of high school and went right to work on the docks. Sometimes I have the feeling that we don't really have very much to talk about. And his ideas about women, I mean they're very old-fashioned. He believes a woman's place is in the home and everything, and he doesn't really think very much of my being an actress. He's proud when I get a part and likes that, but he thinks it's just something for me to amuse myself with until we get married and start making babies."

"And you don't feel that way?"

She gnawed the tip of her index finger. "I don't know exactly *how* I feel, Chip. From the time I was a little girl I wanted to be an actress. It was what I always wanted. After one semester of college I knew I had to get away from classrooms and spend all my time around theaters. But it's so hard. You can't imagine."

"I guess it's very hard to get started."

"It's almost impossible. You saw how many people we had in the theater tonight. Maybe thirty."

"If that."

"I know. It was closer to twenty, and most of them were

58

friends who didn't pay for their tickets. And the actors didn't get paid anything, we're all working for free in the hope that somebody important will see us on stage and have something else for us, and—"

She told me a lot more about what was wrong with trying to act for a living. And then she said, " Sometimes I think I should just forget the whole thing and marry Gordie. That's what he wants me to do. It's a temptation, you know. Just give it all up and have babies and enjoy life. Except I worry that I would wake up some day years from now and wonder what I had done with my life. It's very confusing."

She looked straight into my eyes during this last speech and I felt as though I could see clear through to the back of her head. I found it easy to understand why Gordie was overprotective. There was something about Kim that made you want to put your arms around her and tell her everything was going to be all right. Even if it wasn't.

I was just about to reach across the table and take her hand when something changed on her face. She raised her eyes over my shoulder, then waved a hand. I turned, and of course it was good old Gordie.

He pulled a chair up and sat down. He did not seem overjoyed to see me there. (Which made it mutual, actually.) Kim introduced us, and I found out that he had a last name, McLeod. Then he found out that I was a friend of Melanie's and some of the suspicion left his face. Not all of it, but some.

"You see the play?" I admitted that I had. "Saw it myself a couple of times. Rather catch a movie myself. All these people just talking back and forth. What did you think of Kim?"

"I thought she was very good," I said.

"Yeah, only good thing about the play, far as I'm concerned. She's very talented."

I said she certainly was, or something equally significant.

"But I don't like the people she has to hang around with. It's a well-known fact they're all fairies in that business. A well-known fact. Still in all, as a way for her to pass the time until she settles herself down—"

He went off on a speech that Gloria Steinem would not have

59

enjoyed. I have to admit that I didn't follow it too closely. It was already becoming clear to me that Gordie McLeod and I were never going to become best buddies. I was noting Kim's reactions to what he was saying and trying to figure out just what it was about this ape that attracted her. I had no trouble figuring out what it was about her that appealed to him.

"Well," he said, "it's gettin' to be about that time. Nice meetin' you, guy."

"There was something I wanted to discuss with Kim," I said.

"Oh, yeah?"

"About Melanie," Kim said.

He settled back in his chair. "Well, sure," he said.

"It's a little public here," I said. "Could we go somewhere more private?"

"What for?"

"So that we could talk in private."

"What's this all about, anyway?"

I wasn't making much headway. Kim came to the rescue and suggested we all go back to the apartment. She didn't say *her* apartment or *their* apartment, just *the* apartment. He didn't seem wild about the idea, but we went anyway. He insisted on paying for my coffee. I have to admit I didn't put up a fight.

The apartment, which did turn out to be their apartment, was on Bethune Street a few doors west of Hudson, which made it about equidistant from Kim's theater and the Hudson docks where Gordie did something muscular. It was on the second floor of a good old four-story building. There were three high-ceilinged rooms and a little balcony with a view of nothing spectacular.

There was a good feeling to the apartment, and it was hard to believe Kim had rented it less than a year ago. There were some nice Oriental rugs, a couple of floor-to-ceiling bookshelves, and furniture that was both attractive and comfortable. It was not hard to guess which of the two of them had done the decorating.

Gordie got himself a beer and asked me as an afterthought if I wanted one. I didn't disappoint him by accepting. He sprawled on the couch, took a gurgling swig of beer, and put his feet up. "Let's have it," he said.

60

I started my pitch. That I worked for Leo-Haig-the-Famous-Detective. That Haig and I had uncovered evidence that indicated a strong possibility that Melanie had been murdered. That there were grounds for speculation that Jessica, and perhaps Robin as well, had been similarly done in. That a client who I was not at liberty to name had hired Haig to nail the killer. That it was important to recognize that Caitlin and Kim might be in a certain amount of danger.

And so on.

I didn't get to deliver this entire rap all at once because Gordie kept interrupting. He seemed to find it extremely difficult to follow a simple English sentence and even more difficult to put together one of his own, and he kept turning the conversation onto weird tangents. Earlier, I had found it disturbing that a girl like Kim was thinking about marrying an idiot like Gordie. Now I found it disturbing that she was living with him. What in hell did they talk about?

When I had been able to get it all out, and when Kim had a chance to ask a few questions of her own, Gordie took a last long drink of beer, crumpled the can impressively in one hand, and tossed it unsuccessfully at the wastebasket. "I'll tell you what I think," he said.

I was sure he would.

"What I think, I think it's a load of crap."

"I see," I lied.

"You know what your trouble is, Harrison? You're one of these college boys You read all these books and listened to all these egghead professors and it scrambled your brains."

I didn't say anything.

"Me, I'm an ordinary Joe, you know what I mean? An ordinary man, your average human being. What I mean, I didn't have your advantages. I never even finished high school. I did my learning on the streets."

"So?"

"So I don't look for a complicated answer when there's a simple one staring me in the face. The whole trouble with this country is too many guys like you who went to Harvard and they couldn't recognize crap if they stepped in it."

"I didn't go to Harvard."

"Manner of speaking. Where'd you go? Yale? Princeton?"

"I didn't go to college. I didn't finish high school; I got thrown out in my last year."

"What are you trying to hand me?"

"Nothing in particular, I just—"

"Jesus Christ," he said. "I got no use for college boys, I'll tell you that straight out, but one thing I got less use for is a college boy pretends he's not a college boy. Who do you think you're kidding?"

Enough. "The point is," I said, "that if Kim is in any danger—"

"Kim's not in no danger. And if she is, that's what I'm here for. What are you saying, you're gonna protect her? I mean, I can't see you protecting a pigeon from a cat. No offense, but you get my meaning."

I got his meaning.

"Look," he said, 'I'll be protecting Kim no matter what. This city's a fuckin' jungle; nothing but junkies and spades and fairies and weirdos. But all this murder shit, you're making a mountain out of a mole's hill. Robin, she's in a car and it cracks up. That sound like a murder? How many people go out like that every weekend?"

"Yes, but—"

"Then there's Jessica. She's a dyke and a whore and they're all crazy, so maybe she wasn't getting it regular enough or who knows why, but she goes out the window. Happens all the time. Then there's Melanie, who's some kind of a crazy hippie with drugs and shit and who knows what, and junkies are all the time shoving needles in their arm and winding up dead, you see it every night on television. I mean, let's face it, Kim's the only one in the goddamned family that has anything much on the ball. The older one, Caitlin, she's just a nymphomaniac and a lush. Old man Trelawney must have been pretty sharp to make the score he made, I'll give him that, but he wasn't too good at having kids. Kim's okay but the other four were a batch of sickies."

"They had problems," Kim said. "Don't talk about them like that."

"Look, everybody has problems, kid, but those nuts—"

Kim's eyes flared. "I *loved* Melanie," she said. "And I love Caitlin. I loved all my sisters, and I don't want to hear you *talk* like that about them!"

She stormed out of the room. Gordie's face darkened briefly, then relaxed. "Women," he said. "I'll tell you something, they're all of them a little nuts. They don't have thoughts the way men do. They have feelings. You got to know how to handle them."

After they were married, I knew how he would handle her. He would beat her up whenever he felt she needed it.

"Look," he said, "I want you to stay out of Kim's life. You get me?"

"Huh?"

"I know you got to work your angle like everybody else. You already got a client, you don't need to hang around Kim. I don't want her getting upset."

"I didn't know that I did anything to upset her."

"Seeing you upsets me. And when I get upset Kim gets upset, and I don't want that. You got an angle to work and I can respect that, but I don't want you getting in my way."

"I really want it to be him," I told Haig. "I want it to be him and I want them to bring back capital punishment. Someone has to throw the switch. I volunteer."

"Surely the fact he's living with Kim has nothing to do with your motivation."

"You mean am I interested myself? I don't honestly know. She reminds me of Melanie, and I can't make up my mind whether that turns me on or off. The thing is I *like* her, and I can't see her spending a lifetime with a clown like him. Hell, I can't see her spending a social evening with him."

"But he seems an unlikely suspect."

"I know. I can see him committing murder. I don't think he'd draw the line at something like that. But he wouldn't be so clever in choosing different murder methods. He'd probably just hit each of them over the head."

"I gather he's not enormously intelligent," Haig said dryly.

"He's about as dumb as you can get and still function."

"Is he crafty, though?"

I thought about that. I said, "Yes, I think he is. Animal cunning, that kind of thing."

"He assumed you were 'working an angle.' I submit he so assumed because he's working an angle of his own."

I nodded. "He was more or less telling me to stay off his turf. And he knows about the money. In fact he seems to know a lot about all the sisters. He hasn't been with Kim that long, and they weren't that close."

"That struck me," Haig said. His fingers went to his beard and his eyelids dropped shut. "He knows about the Trelawney money. He wants to marry Kim, to the point where she apparently feels pressured. She hasn't come into the principal of her inheritance yet, of course. And won't for three years." He remained silent for a few minutes. I knew his mind was working, but I had no idea what it was working on. Mine was just sort of treading water.

I got up and went over to watch the African gouramis. There were three half-grown guppies still swimming around. While I watched, the female gourami swam over to one of the guppies but didn't bother devouring it. I guess she wasn't hungry at the moment.

Haig raises several strains of fancy guppies. The species is a fascinating one, and the males of *Lebistes reticulata* are as individual as thumbprints. When they're about half-grown, you can tell (if you're Leo Haig) which ones are going to amount to something. Those you keep.

The others serve as food for other fish. Haig is fond of remarking that the best food for fish is fish, and some of ours require a certain proportion of live food in their diet. We have a pair of leaf fish, for example, who go through a dozen young guppies apiece every day. It used to bother me, the whole idea of purposely raising fish so that you can feed them to other fish, but that's the way Nature does it in the ocean. I used to know a guy who had a pet king snake and used to buy mice and feed them to it. That would bother me a lot more, I think.

"Chip." I turned. "There is a motive lurking here. I keep

getting teasing glimpses of it but I don't have enough hard information to see it. We need to know more about wills and such. Tomorrow—"

But he didn't get to finish the sentence, because just then we heard glass shatter somewhere in the front of the house. We looked at each other, and I started to say something, and then the bomb went off and the whole house shook.

I stood there for a minute. Waiting for the next explosion, probably, but there wasn't one. I went into the front room and saw a crack in one of the front windows.

Then the girls downstairs started shrieking.

7

IT WAS A PIPE BOMB CONSISTING of a length of pipe filled with various goodies, but I'm not going to go into detail. I mean, who knows what lunatic out there might get inspired and follow my directions and bomb a whorehouse on his own? Haig says that Alfred Hitchcock once had a scene in which an assassin used a gun built into a camera, and then a few months after the picture was released someone assassinated somebody just that way, in Portugal I think, and Hitchcock felt very ginchy about it. I can understand that.

What happened was this: someone threw a pipe bomb into the second floor front of our building. That was the broken glass, the sound of the bomb going through the window, which had not been open at the time. Then the bomb went off, shaking the whole house and, more to the point, giving Maria Tijerino and Able-Bodied Seaman Elmer J. Seaton a greater thrill than they could possibly have anticipated.

Shit. I don't want to be cute about this because it was not at all nice. Maria and the sailor were in bed in the front room at the time and the damned bomb blew them to hell and gone. I went in there and looked, God knows why, and then I went into the john and threw up. I mean, I could make a few dozen jokes along the lines of If-you-gotta-go-etc. But the hell with it. I saw it, and it was ugly.

The explosion didn't hurt anybody but Maria and the sailor. It put some cracks in the plaster throughout the house without doing any real structural damage.

It also made some of our fish tanks leak.

Haig and Wong Fat and I missed a lot of the action because we were running around trying to make sure the fish were all right. That probably sounds very callous, but you have to realize that there was nothing we could possibly do for Maria or the sailor. And a leaking fish tank is something that requires attention. If a fish tank absolutely cracks to hell and gone, you can just go to church and light candles for the fish, but we didn't have any that got cracked. The thing is, shock waves will interfere with the structural soundness of an aquarium, which is basically a metal frame with a slate bottom and four glass sides, and quite a few of ours sprung slow leaks, and that meant we had to transfer the fish to sound tanks and empty the leakers before they leaked all over the place. Eventually we would have to repair all the leakers, a process which involves coating all the edges with rubber cement and cursing a lot when the tank leaks anyway.

So while we were scurrying around examining tanks on the third and fourth floor, I gather half the police in Manhattan were stumbling around on the first two floors. There were a couple of ambulances out front and a Fire Department rescue vehicle. There were beat patrolmen and Bomb Squad detectives and God knows who else, and, because it was established that Maria and her sailor were dead, which could not have been too difficult to establish, there were two cops from Homicide.

Yeah.

I suppose you already figured out that it would be the same two cops, Gregorio and Seidenwall. You must have. Because you're reading this, and if I were reading it I would certainly expect to keep encountering the same two cops. (I gather this never happens in real life, but just the other day I read a mystery by Justin Scott called *Many Happy Returns* and the lead character kept cracking up oil trucks, of all things, and each time he turned a truck over the same two humorous cops turned up to glare at him. It didn't seem to matter what part of the city he was in, he always ran into the same goddam cops.)

The thing is, you're reading this in a book, so you know it's Gregorio and Seidenwall again. I wasn't reading it, I was living gamely through it, and they were the last thing I expected.

But there they were.

"... check on the possibility of ..." Gregorio said. I don't know how the sentence had started or how he was planning to end it. He had evidently begun it in the hallway, undeterred by the lack of anyone to hear it, and he didn't end it, because he caught sight of me. "I'll be a ring-tailed son of a bitch," he said.

"Er," I said.

"You again," he said.

You again, I thought.

"I don't like this at all," he said. "A hippie girl OD's in a toilet on the Lower East Side and you're the one who discovers the body. A sailor and a spic hooker fuck themselves into an explosion and you're living upstairs. You know something, Harrison? I'm not crazy about any of this."

"We oughta take him in," Seidenwall said.

"I never believed in coincidence," Gregorio said. "It makes me nervous. I hate to be nervous. I got a stomach that when I get nervous my stomach gets nervous, and I can live without a nervous stomach. I can live better and longer without a nervous stomach."

"We oughta take him in," Seidenwall said.

"I don't like the sense of things fitting together like this," Gregorio said. "How long have you lived in New York, Harrison?"

"A couple of years," I said. "Off and on."

"We oughta take him in," Seidenwall said.

"Off and on," Gregorio said. "A couple of years off and on."

"We oughta take him in."

"A couple of years you were here, and a lot of years I was here, and all that time I never heard of you, Harrison. I never knew you existed. Now I see you twice in two days."

"Three days," I said.

"Shut up," Gregorio said.

"We oughta take him in," Seidenwall said.

Leo Haig said, "Sir!"

And everybody else shut up.

He said, "Sir. You are on my property without my invitation or enthusiastic approval. You have come, as well I can appreciate, to investigate a bombing. You wish to ascertain whether or not the bombing is impinging in any way upon myself and my associates. It is not. We are not involved. The building has been bombed. Living in a building which is sooner or later bombed is evidently a natural consequence of living in the city of New York. It is perhaps an even more natural consequence of living above a house of ill repute. I am not happy about this, sir, as no doubt neither are you. I am distressed, especially as this bombing causes me considerable inconvenience. I am increasingly displeased at your attitude toward my associate, and, by extension, toward myself."

Gregorio and Seidenwall looked down. Leo Haig looked up. Hard. Gregorio and Seidenwall looked away.

Haig said, "Sir. I assume you have no warrant. I further assume your contingency privileges obviate the necessity for a warrant to intrude upon my property. But, sir, I now ask you to leave. You cannot seriously entertain the notion that I or my associate did in fact bomb our own building. We are not witlings. Each of us can vouch for the other's presence at the time of the bombing, as can my associate Mr. Wong Fat." Wong was at that moment cowering under his bed saying the rosary. "You can, sir, as your estimable colleague suggests, take Mr. Harrison into custody. It would be an unutterably stupid act. You could, on the other hand, quit these premises. It appears to me that these are your alternatives. You have only to choose."

I never heard the like. Neither, I guess, did Gregorio. They scooted.

"I always wanted to call someone a witling," Haig said later. "Wolfe does it all the time. I always wanted to do that."

"You did it very well," I said.

"I have my uncle to thank for that," Leo Haig said. "I have my uncle to thank for many things, but one fact sums it all up. But for him, I would have gone through life without ever being able to call a policeman a witling."

We had a beer on the strength of that.

8

I SPENT THE NIGHT IN HAIG'S house. It was late by the time we were done with the fish, even later before we finished talking about the bombing. We agreed that it was possible someone had bombed the whorehouse on purpose, and we also agreed that we didn't believe it had happened that way. That bomb had gone through the wrong window. It had been meant for us, and whoever threw it had his signals crossed.

Which was one of the reasons I spent the night on the couch. Somebody was trying to kill us, and I really didn't want to give him any encouragement.

"You ought to move in here," Haig said over breakfast. "It would expedite matters."

"Not if I have to spend any time on that couch."

"It was uncomfortable?"

"It was horrible," I said. "I kept waking up and wanting to stretch out on the floor, but moving was too painful."

"Of course you'd have a proper bed," Haig said stiffly. "And a proper room of your own, and the implicit right to entertain friends of your own choosing. In addition—"

He paraded the usual arguments. I paid a little attention to them and a lot of attention to breakfast. Corned beef hash, fried eggs, and the world's best coffee. I don't always like coffee all that much, but Wong Fat makes the best I've ever tasted. It's a Louisiana blend with chickory in it and he uses this special porcelain drip pot and it really makes a difference.

After breakfast Haig gave me a list of things to do regarding the fish. Whle I was upstairs attending to them he was on the phone in his office. I finished up and was sitting on my side of the partners' desk at a quarter after eleven. Haig was reading one of Richard Stark's Parker novels. I forget which one. He said, "Formidable," once or twice. I spent ten minutes

70

watching him read. Then he closed the book and leaned back in his chair and played with his beard. After a few minutes of that he took one of his pipes apart. He put it back together again and started to take it apart a second time, but stopped himself.

"Chip," he said.

I tried to look bright-eyed.

"I've made some calls. I spoke with Mr. Shivers and Mrs. Vandiver. Also with several other lawyers. Also with Mr. Bell and a man named LiCastro. Also — no matter. There are several courses of inquiry you might pursue today. You have your notebook?"

I had my notebook.

Indulgence was on the second floor of a renovated brownstone on 53rd Street, between Lexington and Third. The shop on the first floor sold gourmet cookware. I walked up a flight of stairs and paused for a moment in front of a Chinese red door with a brass nameplate on it. There was a bell, and another brass plate instructed me to ring it before opening the door. I followed orders.

The man behind the reception desk was small and precise and black. He had his hair in a tight Afro and wore thick horn-rimmed glasses. His suit was black mohair and he was wearing a red paisley vest with it. His tie was a narrow black knit.

It was air-conditioned in there, but I couldn't imagine how he could have come to work through all that heat in those clothes. And he looked as though he had never perspired in his life.

He asked if he could help me. I said that I wanted to see a girl named Andrea Sugar.

"Of course," he said, and smiled briefly. "Miss Sugar is one of our recreational therapists. Do you require a massage?"

"Uh, yeah."

"Very good. Are you a member?"

I wasn't, but it turned out that I could purchase a trial membership for ten dollars. This would entitle me to the services of a recreational therapist for thirty minutes. I handed over ten of Leo Haig's dollars and he filled out a little

71

membership card for me. When he asked me my name I said "Norman Conquest." Don't ask me why.

"Miss Sugar is engaged at the moment," he said, after my ten dollar bill had disappeared. 'She'll be available in approximately ten minutes. Or you may put yourself in the hands of one of our other therapists. Here are photographs of several of them."

He gave me a little leatherette photo album and I looked through it. There were a dozen photographs of recreational therapists, all of them naked and smiling. In the interests of therapy, I guess. I said I would prefer to wait for Miss Sugar and he nodded me to a couch and went back to his book. It was a collection of essays by Noam Chomsky, if you care.

I sat around for ten minutes during which the phone rang twice. The desk man answered, but didn't say much. I leafed through *Sports Illustrated* and read something very boring about sailboat racing. He went into another room and came back to report that Miss Sugar was waiting for me in the third cubicle on the right. I walked down a short hallway and into a room a little larger than a throw rug. The walls were painted the same Chinese red as the door. The floor was cork tile. The only piece of furniture in the room was a massage table with a fresh white sheet on it.

Andrea Sugar was standing beside the table. She wasn't the girl I had seen at the funeral. She was wearing a white nurse's smock. (I think that's the right word for it.) She was tall, almost my height, and she looked a little like pictures of Susan Sontag. She said hello and wasn't it hot out and other conventional things, and I said hello and agreed that it was hot out there, all right, and she suggested I take off all my clothes and get on the table.

"I'm not really here for a massage," I said.

"You're not supposed to say that, honey,"

"But the thing is—"

"You're here for a massage, sweetie. Your back hurts and you want a nice massage, you just paid ten dollars and for that you'll get a very nice massage, and if something else should happen to develop, that's between you and me, but I'm a

72

recreational therapist and you're a young man who needs a massage, and that's how the rulebook reads. Okay?"

The thing is, I did sort of need a massage. My back still had kinks in it from Leo Haig's corrugated couch. I just felt a little weird about taking all my clothes off in front of a stranger. I don't think I have any particular hangups in that direction, actually, but the whole scene was somehow unreal. Anyway, I took off my clothes and hung them over a wooden thing designed for the purpose and got up on the table and onto my stomach.

"Now," she said. "What seems to be the trouble?"

I guess the question didn't need an answer, because she was already beginning to work on my back. She really knew how to give a back rub. Her hands were very strong and she had a nice sense of touch and knew what muscles to concentrate on. When she got to the small of my back I could feel all the pain of a bad night's sleep being sucked out of the base of my spine, like poison out of a snakebite.

"It's about Jessica Trelawney," I said.

The hands stopped abruptly. "Christ Almighty," she said softly. "Who *are* you?"

"Chip Harrison," I said. "I work for Leo Haig, the detective."

"You're not a cop."

"No. Haig is a private investigator. I was also a friend of Melanie Trelawney's."

"She OD'd the other day."

"That's right."

By now she had gone back to the massage. Her hands moved here and there as we talked, and when they strayed below the belt they began to have an effect that was interesting. I felt an urge to wriggle my toes a little.

"You really didn't come for a massage."

"No, but that doesn't mean you should stop. I came to ask you some questions. If you want me to get dressed—"

"No, that's no good. They look in from time to time and I should be doing what I'm supposed to be doing. You're a friend of Melanie's and you want to ask about Jess?"

"Yes."

"I hope you're trying to find out who murdered her. I just surprised you, didn't I? I never bought that suicide story. Not for a minute. I've never known anyone less suicidal than Jess. She was one of the strongest women I've ever known. How does this feel?"

"Great."

"You've got a nice skin. And you're clean. You wouldn't believe some of the men who come in here. Have you ever had a massage before?"

"No."

"What were we talking about? Jess. No, I never believed she killed herself and I always believed she was murdered. It was a waste of time telling the police this. I was very close to Jess. As a matter of fact we were lovers. I met her in a Women's Lib Group. Consciousness-raising. We responded to each other right away. She had made love with women before, but she had never had a real relationship. We lived together; I moved into her apartment. We bought each other silly little presents. Roll over."

"Pardon?"

"You're done on this side. Roll over onto your back."

I did.

"I got her a job here," she went on. "She didn't have to work, of course. She was rich. But she wanted to work, she didn't like the idea of living off her inheritance and not establishing herself as a person responsible for her own existence. She was extremely tough-minded, Chip."

Her hands were working on my arms and shoulders and chest and stomach. She used a firm touch at first, but as she got further south she switched to a feathery stroking. My mind was not at all interested in sex, for a change, but my body was beginning to display a mind of its own.

I forced myself to talk about Melanie, and how Haig and I were convinced she had been murdered. I didn't go into details and I didn't mention the bombing the night before. I asked her if she had any ideas who might have wanted to kill Jessica.

"Some man," she said.

74

"I meant specifically."

She shook her head and ran her fingers over my thighs. "You meet strange people in this business," she said. "Some very unreal men. The names they'll call a woman when they get off. I don't think they're even conscious of it most of the time. It's automatic, some deep built-in hatred of the entire female sex, and their own sexuality is all mixed up with a desire to dominate and hurt. I had a theory about Jess."

"Tell me."

"Well, it doesn't point anywhere in particular. But I figured she had a client for a massage and he managed to get her home address. He went up there and fucked her and hurt her and then he killed her and threw her out the window. He could have beaten her up, you know. It wouldn't have showed because the fall would have hidden any injuries."

Haig and I had already discussed this. Anything less than a bullet hole would have been consistent with injuries suffered in that great a fall.

"But if Melanie was murdered, then probably it was the same person both times."

"Right," I said.

"I can't think who it could be."

"Possibly someone who stands to gain by killing the five sisters."

"Who stands to gain?"

"It's hard to tell. The money wasn't entailed, it passed over completely to the girls under Cyrus Trelawney's will. Leo Haig is working on it."

"I wish I could help."

We chatted a little more, and then she drew her hands away and I thought the massage was over. I sort of hoped it was. I couldn't take very much more of this.

She said, "It's very warm in here, Chip. Would you mind if I removed my uniform?"

She had a fine body, long and lean and supple. Her breasts were very firm and her stomach perfectly flat. Her skin smelled spicy.

She put her hands right where I hoped she would put them.

She pressed gently, then moved her fingers in that feathery stroke.

"There's one muscle group I haven't been able to relax," she said.

"Yeah. It's sort of embarrassing, if you want to know."

"I'd be embarrassed if you didn't react that way. Would you like me to do something about it?"

"I'd like that."

"You have to tell me what you want me to do."

"Uh."

She was not touching me now. "This isn't part of the standard massage," she explained. "You've had the standard treatment already." I had had the treatment, all right. "If there's anything else you would like, you have to tell me specifically what it is. And then you give me a present because you like me, and I do something very nice for you because I like you, and that's how it's done."

"I see."

"What would you like?"

"Uh. I don't know what the choices are."

"For a small present I could do something manual. For a large present I could do something oral."

"I see."

"You already know I have nice hands. I also have a very nice mouth."

"I'm sure you do."

"I've received lots of compliments on it."

"I'm sure you have."

"So if you'd like to ask me to do something—"

"How much is a small present?"

"Ten dollars would be a small present. Twenty dollars would be a large present. A lot of people give me larger presents than that, but I sort of like you. You're clean and you're not an unpleasant person."

I had about twenty-five dollars with me after paying my trial membership fee. But I was going to have to take cabs and be ready to spend money if the need arose. The twenty dollar present was out of the question and the ten dollar present seemed like a lot of money for a very second-best experience. And I really didn't like the idea of paying for sex. I could almost rationalize this on the grounds that it wouldn't be sex, exactly. I mean, there was nothing really sexual about it, for Pete's sake. It would just be a release from tension. Recreational therapy, you could call it.

What it comes to, really, is that if I had had a hundred dollars in my pocket I would probably have given twenty of them to Andrea. Since I had twenty-five, I told her I was afraid I would have to pass.

"That's cool," she said, slipping back into her uniform. "Maybe you'll drop around again sometime."

"Maybe I will."

"And if there's any way I can help you find out who killed Jess—"

"Maybe there is," I said.

"How?"

"It might help if we knew the names of her customers for the week before she was killed. I don't suppose there would be any connection, but something might turn up."

She gave a low whistle. "That's a tough one. There's no record kept of what guy goes with what girl. They keep track of the number of massages everybody does because you get a percentage of that on top of the presents clients give you. And they keep the names from the membership forms, but you'd be surprised how many men are ashamed to give their right name."

"Not all that surprised, actually."

"I suppose I could find those records, though. For the week before Jessica died? I'll have to be sneaky. You're not supposed to have access to the records. I think they're afraid some of the girls might try a little blackmail. But I'm good at schemes and I shouldn't have much trouble getting around Rastus out there."

My face must have showed something. She laughed. "No, I'm not a racist," she said. "No more than the next bigot, anyway. That's his name."

"You're kidding."

"I don't think he was born with it. But it's his name now and he likes to watch people when he introduces himself. Don't forget your watch, Chip."

The watch I almost forgot told me that it was ten minutes after two when I left Indulgence. I went around the corner and had a cheeseburger and some iced tea. Walking was not a very pleasurable experience at the moment. Andrea Sugar had drained all the pain out of my backbone and rolled it up into a ball and stuffed it into my groin.

I'd given her Leo Haig's number and told her to call as soon as she had the records of clients for the week in question. I couldn't see how it would help, especially since anyone planning to kill Andrea would have likely used a name about as legitimate as old Norm Conquest himself, but it was something to do.

She had always been convinced that Jessica had been murdered. That was the sort of fact Leo Haig usually found interesting and suggestive, so I spent a dime telling him about it. By the time I left the restaurant I could almost walk without limping.

Almost.

9

FERDINAND BELL'S OFFICE WAS within limping distance on the ninth floor of a tall narrow building on 48th Street, just east of Fifth. The building directory in the lobby showed that most of the tenants dealt in stamps or coins. Or both.

In the elevator a man with a European accent said, "I can never recommend for appreciation any surcharges or overprints priced significantly higher than their regular issue counterparts. It is not merely that they may be counterfeited, but that the mere prospect of counterfeiting prevents their reaching their logical levels." I still do not have the slightest idea what he was talking about. I repeated the conversation to Haig, who understands everything, and of course he nodded wisely. He wouldn't tell me what it meant, though.

"If you want to learn about anything under the sun," he said, "you have only to read the right detective story. *The Nine Tailors* will tell you as much as you need to know about bell-ringing in English country churches, for example." (It told me more than I needed to know, to tell you the truth.) " For philately, MacDonald's *The Scarlet Ruse* is excellent. There are others that are less likely to be to your taste—"

"Philately? They were talking about stamps?"

"Of course."

"Well, I didn't know," I said. "How was I supposed to know?"

I haven't read *The Scarlet Ruse* yet. I suppose I'll get to it eventually. The thing is, Haig keeps giving me books to read, and it's impossible to keep up. I did read a couple of books with a coin-collecting background recently, one by Raymond Chandler and another by Michael Innes, so I now know a little more about numismatics than I did when I walked into Ferdinand Bell's office.

He was the man I'd picked out at the funeral as the most likely candidate for the Ferdinand Bell look-alike contest. Today he was wearing a short-sleeved white shirt, open at the throat, and a pair of gray pants that might have been from the suit he'd worn a day ago. They certainly looked as though he had been wearing them for a while.

I had established earlier that he was around forty-seven. He looked both older and younger, depending on how you looked at him. He was plump, with chipmunk cheeks and happy little eyes, and that made him appear younger than he was, but his hair (short and snow white, with a slightly receding hairline) added a few years to his appearance. He sat on a stool behind a row of glass showcases in which coins rested on top of two-by-two brown envelopes. There was a bookcase to his right, filled to capacity, and a desk to his left with a great many books and magazines piled sloppily on it.

He looked up when I entered, which I guess is not too surprising, and he blinked rapidly when I told him who I was.

"Yes, Mr Haig called me. So I've been awaiting you. But somehow I expected an older man. Aren't you a little young to be a detective? And didn't I see you at the funeral?"

I gave him a qualified yes. Since I wasn't officially a detective the first question was hard to answer. And the second was impossible; I had been at the funeral, and I saw him there, but how did I know whether he saw me?

"Have a seat," he said. "Or should we go somewhere and have a cup of coffee? But I don't think we'll be disturbed here today. My Saturdays are usually quiet. I tend to mail orders and such matters. That's if I'm not out of town working a convention. The A.N.A. is coming up in two weeks. It's in Boston this year, you know."

I didn't. I also didn't know what the A.N.A. was, but I've since learned. It's the American Numismatic Association, and it's the most important coin convention of the year. He went on to tell me that he had a bourse table reserved and expected to be bidding on some choice lots in the auction. Large cents, I think he said.

"I understand you believe Melanie was murdered," he said.

"I'm reading between the lines there. Your Mr. Haig was deliberately vague. Dear me, I've made an unintentional rhyme, haven't I? *Your Mr. Haig/Was deliberately vague.* And I gather you have a client in this matter?"

"Yes."

"I don't suppose you could tell me who it is?"

Haig had said I could, and so I did. I told him one of them, anyway.

"Caitlin! Extraordinary."

I wanted to ask him why it was extraordinary. Instead I started asking him some questions about his wife, Robin. Had she seemed at all nervous in the weeks immediately preceding her death? Had her behavior changed in any remarkable way?

He squinted in concentration and I swear his nose twitched like a bunny's. "As if she had some precognitive feelings about her fate? I never thought of that."

"Or as if she were afraid someone would murder her."

"Dear me. Now *that's* a speculation I've never entertained. Just let me think now. Do you know, I can't even concentrate on her attitude then because the whole idea of her having been murdered is so startling to me."

I nodded.

"Naturally I blamed myself for her death. After all, I was driving. I have a tendency to let my mind wander when I drive. Especially when tired, and I *was* tired that day; it had been a grueling weekend." He leaned forward and pressed his forehead with the fingertips of one hand. "I had never had an accident before. My woolgathering never seemed to interfere with my driving. Although I could never help thinking that if I had been paying a bit more attention to what I was doing I might have seen that patch of ice." He moved his hand to shade his eyes. "And Robin might be alive today."

I didn't say anything for a minute or two. He wiped his eyes with the back of his hand and straightened up on his stool. He forced his smile back in place.

A wistful look came into his eyes. "There's something I've always wondered about, Chip. May I call you that?"

"Sure."

"Something I've always wondered about. That skid I took. I grew up in an area where winter was long and severe. I learned to drive on snow and ice, how to react to sudden skids. Not to fight the wheel, to turn with the skid, all of those actions that are contrary to instinct and must consequently be learned and reinforced. And on the day of the accident I reacted as I had been trained to react."

"But it didn't work."

"No, it did not. And I've wondered if there couldn't have been a possibility of mechanical failure involved. I had the car looked at. It wasn't damaged all that severely, and if Robin had been sitting beside me and wearing a belt—" His face darkened. He bit his lip and went on. "They found that the steering column was damaged. I had never thought before that it might have been tampered with. Now I find myself wanting to seize on the possibility to whitewash my own role in the affair. If the car had been sabotaged, if some fiend intentionally caused that accident—"

He got to his feet. "You must excuse me," he said. "I have a nervous stomach. I'll be a few moments. You might like to have a look at the coins in that case. There are some nice Colonials."

I had a look at the Colonials. I couldn't really tell you if they were nice or not. I also had a look at the books on his desk and in the glass-fronted bookcase. They all seemed to be about coins, which probably stood to reason. Some of them looked very old.

I was thumbing through a book called *The United States Trade Dollar*, by John Willem, when Bell came back. "An illuminating book," he said over my shoulder. "The Trade dollar was coined purely to facilitate commerce in the Orient. The Chinese traders would put their personal chop marks on them to attest to their silver value. I've a few pieces in stock if you'd care for a look at the genuine article."

He showed me three or four coins, returned them to their little brown envelopes and put them away. "My library is my most important asset," he said. "There's a motto in professional numismatics — Buy the book before the coin. The wisest sort of advice and all too few people follow it. Numismatics is a science, not just a matter of sorting change and filling holes in a Whitman folder. Take those Trade dollars. The whole history of the China trade is waiting to be read there."

He went on like that for a while. I tend to look interested even when I'm not, which Haig tells me is an asset; people reveal more of themselves to people who appear interested. So I listened, and it really was pretty interesting, but it wasn't getting me any closer to the man who killed Melanie and tried to bomb Leo Haig's house.

I found an opportunity to get the conversation back on the rails and brought up the question of motive. "Suppose someone did sabotage your car. He couldn't have been certain of killing just Robin. He would have had a shot at killing you, too."

"That had occurred to me."

"Well, anyone who's busy killing off five sisters probably wouldn't draw the line at including someone else here and there. Who benefited by Robin's death?"

"Financially?" He shrugged his shoulders. "That's no secret, surely. Except for a few minor bequests, I inherited Robin's entire estate."

"But suppose you had both been killed in the accident."

'Dear me. I hadn't thought of that. I'd have to check that, but it seems to me that I recall a provision to cover my dying before Robin. It would also cover simultaneous death, I presume. It's my recollection that the estate would be divided among her surviving sisters."

"I see."

"I'd have to check, but that would present no difficulty. My lawyer has a copy of Robin's will. I could call him first thing Monday morning. Just let me make a note of that."

He made a note of it, then looked up suddenly. "I say, Chip. You don't think I ought to consider myself in danger now, do you?" He laughed nervously. "It's hard to take seriously, isn't it? But if it *ought* to be taken seriously—"

"Do you have a will?"

"Yes, of course. I drew up a new will shortly after Robin's death. A few thousand dollars to a couple of numismatic research foundations, some smaller charitable bequests, and the balance to my sister in Lyons Falls."

"And you inherited Robin's estate free and clear?"

"Yes. Shortly after we were married we drew wills leaving everything to one another absolutely without encumbrance." His eyes clouded. "I expected it would be my will which would be put to the test first. I was seventeen years Robin's senior. She preferred older men, you know. Her first husband was as old as I am now when she married him. There's a history of heart trouble in my family. I naturally expected to predecease Robin, and although I hadn't all that much to leave her I wanted my affairs to be in order."

I told him I didn't think he was in any danger. No one could now expect to profit from his death. The news didn't cheer him much. He was too caught up in thoughts of his dead wife.

I asked if he knew anything about Jessica's will. "I barely knew Jessica," he said. "The Trelawney sisters were not close, and Robin and I kept pretty much to ourselves. Most of our close friends were business associates of mine. Coin dealers are gregarious folk, you know. We hardly regard one another as competitors. Often we do more business buying from each other and selling to each other than we do with actual collectors. No, I don't know anything about Jessica's will. I did go to her funeral, just as I went to Melanie's. I don't honestly know why I attended either of them. I had little enough to say to anyone there. I suppose it was a way of preserving my ties to Robin." He lowered his eyes. "We had so little time together."

"How did you meet her? Was she interested in coins?"

"Oh, not at all. Although she did come to share some of my interest during our life together. She was growing interested in love money, those little pins and brooches made of three-cent pieces, a very popular jewelry form of the mid-nineteenth century. I would always pick up pieces for her when I saw them. No real value, of course, but she liked them." He smiled at some private memory. "How did I meet her? I was a friend of her first husband, Phil Flanner. I suppose I fell in love with

Robin while she was married to him, although I honestly didn't realize it at the time. Phil died tragically; a stupid accident. I began seeing her not too long after the funeral. I was drawn to her and enjoyed her company, still not recognizing what I felt as love. Gradually we both came to realize that we were in love with one another. I wish we had realized this sooner, so that we might have been married sooner. We had so very little time."

10

WHEN I GOT BACK TO THE HOUSE on 20th Street, Haig was on the top floor playing with his fish, repairing the leakers with rubber cement. When I asked if he wanted me to help, he grunted. I stopped in the kitchen where Wong was hacking a steak into bite-sized pieces with a cleaver. I left without a word. When he's chopping things he looks positively dangerous and I try to stay out of his way. I went downstairs and talked a little with some of the girls.

"Why they wanna blow up Maria?" Carmelita wanted to know. "She don' never hurt nobody. One guy, he say she give him a clop, but Maria never give nobody no clop. He get his clop somewhere else. Maria tell him, you get your clop from your mother, she say."

That was even more of a down than watching Haig swearing at his fish tanks, so I went over to Dominick's and had a beer and watched the Mets find a new way to lose. Matlack had a one-run lead going into the bottom of the ninth, struck out the first man, hit the second man on the arm, and got the third man to hit a double-play ball to short.

That was his mistake. They had Garrett playing short and he made the play without the ball. The ball went to left field and the runners went to second and third, and somebody walked and Bobby Bonds hit a 2-2 pitch off the fence and Dominick turned the set off.

"Shit," he said.

So I went back and read a couple of chapters of an old Fredric Brown mystery until Haig came down, and then I gave him a full report. He made me go over everything a few hundred times. Then he closed his eyes and fiddled with his beard and put his head back and said "Indeed" fifteen times and "Curious" eighteen times. He wouldn't tell me what was curious.

I spent most of the night walking around the Village looking for somebody to sleep with. It was hotter than hell and there wasn't much air in the air. I didn't have any luck. I have a feeling I wasn't trying very hard. I had a couple of beers and a few cups of coffee and called Kim a couple of times, but no one answered.

I went back to my room and played a Dylan record over and over. I remember thinking that a little grass would be nice and regretting having flushed it to oblivion. It was a rotten night. I had run all over town and hadn't accomplished anything much. I was sorry I hadn't spent twenty of Haig's dollars on a massage and realized I would have been just as sorry if I had.

I thought about going downstairs to give Kim one more call, and I decided the hell with it, and eventually I went to sleep.

Nothing much happened Sunday. I slept late and had breakfast around noon and walked over to Haig's house because I couldn't think of anything else to do. I got there in time to watch Wong devastate him at backgammon. Wong beats hell out of me, but that was nothing compared to the way he routed Haig. It was pathetic to watch.

"There's nothing for you to do," he said.

Which would have been all right except that I felt like doing something. I hung around for a while and did some routine maintenance on the fish, although Sunday was supposed to be a free day for me. Just before dinner I called Andrea Sugar at home to find out if she had managed to get the records. She wasn't in. I called her a couple of hours later and reached her and learned that she hadn't had a chance to do anything yet.

I read a couple of books at Haig's. After dinner I caught a movie. I don't remember which one.

On the way home I stopped at a pay phone and called Kim. I was a little worried about her, if you want to know. I also just found myself thinking about her a lot. I asked her if she had thought of anything significant, or if anybody had been following her or anything. She had nothing to report.

"The thing is," I said, "I'd like to go over things with you sometime. When Gordie's working or something, if you follow me."

"I think I follow you."

"Because he's not exactly crazy about me, and it's hard to get anyplace with him around. I mean as far as a conversation is concerned."

"He's here right now. He's in the other room. I don't think I'll tell him it's you on the phone."

"That sounds like a good idea."

"He'll be working tomorrow from noon to eight. I have a couple of classes during the afternoon, but the evening's clear."

"Don't you have a performance?"

"Monday's the dark night off-Broadway. Anyway, the play closed today."

"I'm sorry to hear that."

"Well, it wasn't very good. The critics hated it. Would you want to come over around six tomorrow?"

I said I would.

I went home and decided Gordie was the killer and that meant Kim was safe. He wouldn't kill her now. First he would kill Caitlin, and possibly her husband as well, and then he would marry Kim, and *then* he would kill her.

Monday there were things for me to do and places for me to go, so of course it rained. Haig had made appointments for me all over the place. I had to see a couple of lawyers, one on Fifth Avenue and one near City Hall just a block from Addison Shivers. I decided to drop in on him and let him know how we were doing, but he was in conference with a client when I got there. I went out and had fish and chips for lunch and dropped in on him again, but this time he was out having lunch, so I said the hell with it and took the subway uptown as far as Canal Street, which is not all that far. I walked up Mulberry to the address Haig had given me.

It didn't look like a place where I was going to feel tremendously welcome. It was the Palermo Social and Recreation Club, and there were a couple of old men playing bocce over to the right, and two other men sitting over a lackadaisical game of dominoes, and a fifth man watching the curl of lemon peel swim around in his cup of espresso. They all looked at me when I walked in. There was no discernible gleam of welcome in their eyes.

I went to the man sitting alone and asked him if he was John LiCastro. He asked who wanted to know, and I told him who I was and who I worked for and he smiled with the lower half of his face and pointed to a chair. I sat down and he told me I was privileged to work for a great man.

I agreed with him, but I wasn't too sure of this at the moment, because it was beginning to seem to me that the great man was not accomplishing a whole hell of a lot. The great man had not left the house yet, which certainly gave him a lot in common with Nero Wolfe, but neither had the great man called any suspects together, or even established that there *were* any suspects, for Pete's sake. The great man was spending a lot of time on his fish while I was keeping the New York Subway System out of the red, or trying to.

I didn't say any of this to Mr. LiCastro. I had a pretty good feeling that it was extremely unintelligent to say anything to Mr. LiCastro that Mr. LiCastro didn't want to hear. I told him what I had been instructed to tell him, and asked him what I had been instructed to ask him, and he took in my words with little darting affirmative movements of his head. At one point his eyes narrowed as he fixed on some private thought, and I realized that I was sitting across the table from a man who could kill a man at five o'clock and sit down to a huge dinner at five-thirty and not even worry about indigestion.

Then he ordered espresso for both of us and leaned back in his chair and asked some questions of his own, and there was a warm glow in his eyes and a look of complete relaxation on his face.

It was really something to see.

"So LiCastro is crazy about tropical fish," I said later. "I was wondering how on earth you would know somebody like him. His discus spawned, but a fungus got the eggs."

"That usually happens."

"He was tickled enough that he got them to spawn in the first place. He's trying a new fungicide and he wants your opinion of it. He didn't remember the name. He's going to call you later."

"And he'll make some inquiries about Gordon McLeod?"

"That's what he said. I had a very eerie feeling about that. I wanted to make sure he just made inquiries. I thought he might think I was asking for something more serious than inquiries. Like he might have thought I was being subtle and indicating you wanted McLeod killed if I didn't spell things out."

"I doubt it."

"Well, I wasn't sure. Also I had the feeling that if you did want McLeod killed, and you said as much to LiCastro, then that would be the end of McLeod."

"That I do not doubt," Haig said. "Continue."

I continued. "Jessica Trelawney drew a will a couple of weeks after Robin died. I have the date written down if it matters."

"It may."

"Her lawyer says that's a common response to the death of someone else. He also says she left everything to a feminist group called Radicalesbians. I'm not making this up. He is sure the will is going to be challenged by attorneys for Caitlin Vandiver, and he told me off the record that he's just as sure it won't stand up. He more or less implied that he drew it in such a way as to make it easy to challenge. I'm pretty sure he's not a big fan of Radicalesbians."

"Indeed."

"So no one stood to gain a penny by Jessica's death, except for Radicalesbians, but that doesn't prove anything because no one necessarily knew about her will. Before that she had never drawn a will, and if she had died intestate, everything would have been divided among the surviving sisters. Which is what would have happened to Robin's money if she and Bell had died together in the car accident."

"Car wreck," Haig said.

"Indeed," I said.

"Precision is important. Language is a tool, its edge must be kept sharp."

90

"Indeed. Melanie did die intestate, which is a word I have now used twice in two minutes and can't remember ever using before. I suppose it's a part of keeping the edge of my tool sharp. So her money will be divided among Caitlin and Kim, and—"

"Between."

"Huh?"

"One divides among three persons and between two. I don't like to keep correcting you, Chip."

"I can tell you don't. I found out who Caitlin's lawyer is, but couldn't reach him."

"He wouldn't divulge information about her will anyway."

"He probably will, because it's Addison Shivers, but I couldn't get to see him. Anyway, I figured he would tell us or not tell us over the phone. I would guess that her money is scheduled to go to her husband, but you can't be sure, can you? I mean, she changes husbands pretty quickly, and if she's not morbid she might not want to have to change her will that frequently. The problem is that I keep going out after information and I keep getting it and it doesn't seem to get me anywhere."

"Sooner or later everything will fit into place."

"By that time everyone could be dead."

"In the long run everyone always is, Chip." He began filling a pipe, tamping down each pinch of tobacco very carefully. "We have to make haste slowly," he went on, while making haste slowly with the pipe. "We are making progress. We are in the possession of data we previously lacked. That is progress."

"I suppose."

"There are cases that lend themselves to Sherlockian methodology. Cases which are solved by the substance in a man's trouser turnups. Cases which hinge on a dog's silence in the night or the chemical analysis of coffee grounds." He closed his eyes and put the deliberately filled pipe back in the pipe rack. His hand went to his beard and he leaned back in his chair. "This, I think, is another sort of case entirely. There is someone somewhere with a logical reason to kill the five daughters of Cyrus Trelawney. He had a reason to sabotage Ferdinand Bell's car, a reason to pitch Jessica Trelawney out a window, a reason to inject Melanie Trelawney with a fatal overdose of heroin. If we determine the reason, we will have determined the killer."

He sat forward suddenly, and his eyes opened like those dolls that go sleepy-bye when you lay them down on their backs. "Do you know something, Chip? I think there's an element of Ross MacDonald in this. I can't avoid the feeling that the underlying motive is buried somewhere deep in the past. As though it all has its roots forty years ago, in Canada."

"Canada?"

"A figure of speech. So often Lew Archer uncovers something that started forty years ago in Canada, you know." He spun around in his chair and gazed at the rasboras. They didn't seem at all self-conscious. While he let them provide inspiration, I took out my nail file and cleaned out the dirt from under my fingernails. I only tell you this so you won't think I was just sitting there doing nothing.

He turned around again, eventually, and folded his hands on his round belly. He looked elfin but determined. "I shall call Addison Shivers," he said. "I have some questions to ask him."

He reached for the telephone, and it rang. So he picked it up, naturally enough. It doesn't seem to surprise him much when things like this happen. In fact he made it look as though he had been waiting for it to ring.

He talked briefly, mostly saying things like "Yes", and "Indeed." Then he hung up and raised his eyebrows at me.

"Our client," he said.

"Mr. Shivers?"

"Mrs. Vandiver. She's at her house on Long Island. She wants to see you immediately. She says it's rather urgent."

11

YOU GET TO SANDS POINT BY TAKING the Long Island Rail Road
to the Port Washington stop. I understand that there are people
who do this every day. What I don't understand is why.

I got on the train at Penn Station, and got off it at Port
Washington. I stood there on the platform for a minute, and
a very tall and very thin man came up to me. "You would be
Mr. Harrison," he said.

"I would," I said. "I mean, uh, I am. Yes."

"I am Seamus," he said. "I've brought the car."

The car was a Mercedes, about the size of Chicago. I started
to get in the front next to Seamus, but stopped when he gave
me a very disappointed glance. I closed the door and got in the
back instead. He seemed happier about this.

There was a partition between the front and rear seats, which
kept Seamus and me from having to make small talk to each
other. I sat back and looked out the window at one expensive
home after another. Finally, we turned onto what I thought was
a side road but turned out to be the Vandiver driveway. It
wandered through a stand of old trees and finally led to a house.

The house gave you an idea of what God could have done if
he'd had the money. That's not my line; I read it somewhere,
but I can't think of a way to improve on it. There were these
Grecian columns in front which you would think no house
could live up to, and then the house went on to overpower the
columns, and it was all about as impressive as anything I've ever
seen. Caitlin and Melanie had each inherited the same amount
of money, and Caitlin lived here, while Melanie had lived in
Cockroach Heaven, and it wasn't hard to feel that Caitlin had
a better appreciation of creature comfort.

She was waiting for me in a room carpeted in white shag and
decorated in what I think they call French provincial. The

furniture did not come from the Salvation Army. There were oil paintings on the walls, including one that I recognized as a portrait of Cyrus Trelawney.

"I'm so glad you're here," she said. "It's been such a bore of a day. Your drink is Irish whiskey, if I remember correctly. Straight, with a soda chaser?"

It was the last thing I wanted, but I evidently had an image to maintain. She made the drinks, fixing herself a massive Martini, and her eyes sparkled as we touched our glasses together. "To crime," she said.

I took a sip and avoided coughing. I'm sure it was excellent whiskey, but at that point it tasted a lot like shellac.

"I hope you didn't mind my sending Seamus for you," she said. "He's not really a chauffeur. He's more of a general houseman. I usually prefer to do my own driving, actually, but I hate waiting for anything. Especially trains, and the Long Island is hardly ever in on time. Did you have a dreadful ride?"

"It wasn't too bad."

"You were sweet to come. And your Mr. Haig does inspire confidence, doesn't he? It put my mind at rest just to talk to him for a few minutes."

"He's quite a man," I said.

She moved closer to me and put her hand on my arm. She was wearing the same perfume she had worn at the funeral. Her blouse was a black and white print and it was cut low in front. She was not wearing a bra.

"Let's step outside," she said. "Did it rain in the city? We had quite a storm out here this morning and it's actually cooled things off a bit. It's rather pleasant outside."

We took our drinks and walked through some paths in back of the house to a little garden walled in by oaks and beeches. Caitlin sat down on the grass and kicked her shoes off. I stood there for a moment, then sat down next to her.

"I gather there was something you wanted to tell me," I said.

"Oh?"

"Mr. Haig said you told him it was urgent."

She nodded solemnly. "I said it was rather urgent that I see you."

94

"That's what he said."

"Because I felt an urgent need to see you, Chip." She finished her drink and set the glass down on the lawn. She sat back, her arms out behind her to support her weight, and her breasts strained against the black and white blouse. "I felt quite bored," she said. "And quite lonely."

"I see."

"Do you? And of course I wanted a first-hand report on the case. Do you really think someone wants to murder me?"

"It looks that way."

"But why?"

"That's what we're trying to find out." It occurred to me that this would be a good time to find out about her will. "Haig says motive is the big question. He wants to know who would benefit from your death."

"Practically everyone, I imagine. I'm a very wicked woman, Chip."

"Uh."

"You have no idea just how wicked I can be. But of course, you're talking about my will. It's very straightforward, actually. Gregory and I made wills in each other's favor at the time of our marriage. Whichever of us goes first, the other picks up all the marbles."

"I see."

"But I really don't think Greg would murder me, do you? Or if he did, it wouldn't be for money or anything so vulgar. He might kill me out of justifiable rage. I do behave rather badly, you know." She ran her tongue over her lips. This is a very trite gesture, but she made it work anyway. "I suppose I could change my will and leave everything to Radicalesbians like my brilliant sister Jessica. Did you hear about that?"

"I just saw her lawyer today."

"What a dimwitted dyke she was. Not that I have anything against lesbians myself. I think they limit themselves, that's all. Like vegetarians."

"Vegetarians?"

"Vegetables are nice, but so is meat."

"Oh."

"And girls are nice, but so are men." She smiled softly. "I went through a gay period myself in my girlhood. I think I may have mentioned it to you the other day."

"Uh, sort of."

"I was in school at the time. There was this girl who was absolutely mad for me. She was a pretty thing, very small and dark, not like me physically at all. Her breasts just filled my hands. I liked that. She, on the other hand, was partial to large breasts. Do you like large breasts, Chip?"

"Uh, sure."

"I thought you probably did. She told me one day what she wanted to do to me. She wanted to lick me here." She indicated with her hand where the other girl had wanted to lick her. "So I let her. It was such heaven. She didn't insist that I do anything in return, but do you know something, Chip? I discovered that I wanted to. I suppose it was curiosity at first, but I found I enjoyed it very much. Going down on her, that is."

"Er."

"I liked the taste. I'll tell you something fascinating. At the time I only thought girls did it to each other. I didn't imagine that a man would want to do it. But I've since learned that some men enjoy it very much. Have you ever done it?"

"Yes."

"Do you enjoy doing it?"

"Yes."

"I rather thought you might." She opened the top buttons of her blouse. Her skin was creamy and flawless. "But to get back to what I was saying," she said. "About lesbians and how limited they are. Now I adored eating my little friend, you understand, but then I went to bed with an older man and he taught me ever so many things, and while I still found girls amusing, I certainly wasn't about to go without men for the rest of my life. Do you know what I particularly enjoyed?"

"What?"

"Fellatio."

"Oh."

"It's such a technical term for such an intimate act, isn't it?"

"I never thought about it."

"You never thought about fellatio?"

"I never thought about the, uh, term, uh."

"Such an intimate act," she said. Her hand was on my thigh now. "I'm mad for penises. Isn't that terrible of me? I like to feel them grow in my mouth. Oh, but yours has already grown, hasn't it? Oh, lovely. Lovely."

I took her by the shoulders and kissed her. Her mouth tasted of gin and tobacco and honey, and her perfume wrapped me up like a blanket. Her hand kept doing great things while we kissed.

She said, "This is a very private place, Chip. No one can see us here. We can take off all our clothes and roll around in the grass all we want."

We took off all our clothes and rolled around in the grass a lot. Her body was delicious, taut and sleek and smooth, and if there was any age worn into it, I couldn't tell you about it. We did a whole host of things I somehow don't feel compelled to tell you about, and then she decided that she wanted to conclude with the thing she particularly enjoyed.

"I can taste myself on you," she said. "I like that."

Then she didn't say anything any more, and neither did I, and it was a lot like going to heaven without the aggravation of dying first.

I'll tell you something. It was pretty embarrassing to write that last scene. According to Haig, the less sexual detail in these books, the better. "Archie Goodwin very obviously leads an active sex life," he says, "but he does no more than allude to it. He doesn't throw it in your face, doesn't drag you into various bedchambers with him."

But Mr. Elder says times have changed, and that if we expect him to publish these books, there better be a lot of screwing in them. "You've got to arouse the reader," he said. "The reports on the murders and what an interesting character Haig is, that's all fine, but you've got to turn the reader on in this day and age. And of course you've got to do it in good taste."

I don't know if I turned you on, and I don't know if it was in good taste or not. I have to admit I turned myself on just now,

97

though. Just remembering how terrific it was.

A while later we were back in our clothes. We were also back in the room with the white shag carpet, and Caitlin was drinking another jumbo Martini. I had turned down the Irish whiskey in favor of a Dr. Pepper with a lot of ice.

"Oh, my," she said. "That was quite wonderful, wasn't it? I have a confession to make, Chip. I lured you out here for no other reason than to seduce you. Do you think you can possibly forgive me?"

I said I thought I probably could.

"You're such a charming boy, you know. And terribly attractive, and I've been wanting to take you to bed ever since our lunch together." She stretched like a waking cat. "And it's so deadly dull out here. There's Seamus, of course, but when one has sex with one's servants one is limited to the more conventional approaches. It is considered terribly déclassé to perform fellatio upon the domestic help. Now if only I were Jewish, I could blow my chauffeur all I wanted."

That's a pun. Maybe you already knew that. I didn't, and so I didn't laugh, which must have annoyed Caitlin a little. The idea is that Jews have a trumpet made out of a ram's horn which they blow in synagogue on certain holy days, and it's called a *shofar*.

We talked about various things, most of them at least slightly sexual, and I had another Dr. Pepper while she had another Martini, and then I remembered that I had an appointment to see Kim around six. I mentioned this and Caitlin glanced at her watch.

"Hell," she said. "I'd planned on driving you back to the city myself."

"I can take a train."

"No, you wouldn't want to do that. One trip on the Long Island is as much as should be required of anyone. I wanted to drive you, but Gregory's due home soon and he likes me to be here when he arrives. I can't imagine why. I'll have Seamus drive you."

"You really don't have to bother."

98

"It's no bother," she said. "I've no use for him around here at the moment." She picked up the telephone and made a bell ring in another part of the house. When Seamus answered, she told him to bring the car around in a few minutes.

I kissed her a few times and told her not to worry about the murderer, which was silly in view of the fact that she could not have been worrying less about the murderer. Then we went out and stood on the porch and watched Seamus drive the car almost fifteen feet before it exploded.

I was going to write that it was like nothing I had ever seen before, but of course I'd seen it a hundred times in a hundred movies. That's just what it looked like. All of a sudden the car went up into the air and came down in pieces. Most of the pieces were metal, but some of them were Seamus, and they were raining down all over the lawn. One hunk of metal actually landed within a few yards of us, and we were standing half a football field away from the car when it blew up.

"Oh Christ," Caitlin kept saying. "Oh Christ."

I didn't know what to do first. The police would have to be called, obviously, but the most immediate problem was Caitlin. She was shaking and all the color was gone from her face and she looked ready to pass out. I got her inside and tried to make her sit down, but her body went rigid.

"You have to fuck me," she said.

I stared at her, but she was already getting out of her clothes. "I have to have it right now, right now. I have to, you have to do it for me, that could have been me in that car, somebody planted a bomb to kill me, somebody wants to murder me. It's true, it's really true. Christ, you have to fuck me, you just have to."

I was positive I wouldn't be able to. I mean, watching a car blow up isn't normally my idea of a turn-on. But they say that a close escape from death makes you want to reaffirm the fact that you're alive in a sexual way, and it had crossed my mind that it could have been me in the car when it blew up, too, and I guess that made the difference. I got out of my clothes in a hurry, got down on the white shag rug with her, and we began

99

screwing like minks, which is a vulgar way to put it, I guess, but that's what we were doing.

I never heard the door open. I may have left it open, as far as that goes. I don't think I would have heard an earthquake at that point. It was very basic and intense and without frills, and I don't suppose much time elapsed from start to finish, but the finish was a good one and I lay there on top of her wondering if my heart would ever go back to beating at its usual rate, and a man's voice said, "Caitlin, I believe I'm entitled to an explanation."

"He has always had an instinct for disastrous timing," she said in my ear. "Always."

"Caitlin—"

"At least he refrained from speaking until we finished," she went on. "Breeding tells, after all. That's something."

"I come home from work," Gregory Vandiver said reasonably. "I return to my house at my usual hour. I find my car blown to bits all over my lawn; I find my manservant dead in the wreckage and I find my wife copulating with some strange young man on the middle of the drawing room floor. Now *wait* a minute. I've seen you before, haven't I? Yes, I daresay I have. Don't tell me, it'll come to me in a minute."

12

BETWEEN THE SANDS POINT POLICE and the Long Island Rail Road, it was almost ten o'clock before I got back to the city. I did manage to call Kim before that, from the station in Port Washington, but it probably would have been better if I hadn't called her at all. I didn't manage to say three sentences to her before Gordie took the phone away from her.

"You take a lot of telling," he said. "I don't want you coming here, I don't want you calling here, I don't want you sticking your nose in where it ain't wanted." Then he told me to do something I wouldn't have been able to do if I had wanted to, which I didn't in the first place, and then he slammed the phone down.

I walked from Penn Station to Haig's house. I had given him a little of it earlier over the phone and now I gave him the whole thing in detail. (I left out the sex part, at least as far as going into details was concerned. I mean, I had to let him know that Gregory Vandiver walked in and found me screwing his wife. That was the kind of thing that might turn out to be pertinent. So I told him what I had done, you might say, without telling him how much I had enjoyed it.)

"The timing," he said, "is very critical here."

"Right. The killer had about an hour and a half to plant the bomb. The car was all right when Seamus picked me up at the station."

"Indeed."

"She usually did her own driving. Anybody who knew her well would probably know that."

"Do the police know that?"

"No. The police think that the killer did what he was trying to do. It seems that Seamus was involved with some faction of the I.R.A. The police had a sheet on him because he was

101

suspected of playing a role in a gun-running operation. So they think Seamus was the intended victim, and they also think they have several leads."

"I take it you and the Vandivers permitted them to continue thinking this."

"Yes."

"I'm not sure that was wise."

"Neither am I, but it seemed like a good idea at the time. I was passed off as a friend of Mrs. Vandiver's who happened to be visiting at the time. Her husband could have confirmed that we were friendly."

"Indeed."

"Gordie McLeod was back in the Village by eight-fifteen. Because I talked to him on the phone, and no, it wasn't my idea. I wanted to talk to Kim, but he included himself in. Of course he didn't have to stick around while a batch of Long Island public employees asked dumb questions and took pictures of everything, but I'm sure he was at work all day."

"He was not."

"Oh?"

"Mr. LiCastro called. The fungicide he wants to use will render the discus spawn infertile. I so informed him and gave him some suggestions. Gordon McLeod did not show up today for what I believe is called a shape-up. Mr. McLeod has been betting on quite a few horses lately. With little success."

"That's interesting."

"It is. Nor is he in debt to his bookmaker. His losses, however, have of late exceeded his wages, and yet he has been consistently able to settle his debts promptly, and in cash."

"He must be sponging off Kim."

"Perhaps. It would be useful to determine this."

I nodded. Haig put his feet up on the desk. He tries this every once in a while, but he's always uncomfortable because his legs are too short and his abdomen too large. He gave it up after a few seconds.

He said, "I had a visitor during your absence. Mr. Ferdinand Bell."

"What did he want?"

"To be helpful. A noble ambition, but I'm not sure he achieved its realization. He described the swerving of his automobile with an excess of detail. Listening to him, I very nearly felt that I was in it at the time. It was not a feeling I particularly enjoyed."

"Did he have anything else to say?"

"He had some things to say about Miss Andrea Sugar. He brought to my attention the possibility that a lesbian relationship might have existed between her and Jessica Trelawney."

"No kidding."

"He seemed shocked by this. I find his shock more interesting than the relationship itself, certainly. He also said that Mr. Vandiver is in serious financial difficulties."

"You couldn't prove it by the house."

"So I gather. Mr. Vandiver has apparently suffered some financial reverses."

"How would Bell know that?"

"I'm not sure he knew that he knew it. He was letting his mind wander in my presence, talking generally about the flightiness of the sisters Trelawney. Jessica's homosexuality, Melanie's hippie life style, Kim's hour upon the stage—"

"Kim seems pretty straight-headed to me."

"Your bias on the subject has already been noted. He also alluded to Caitlin's liberated sexuality, which he cloaked with the euphemism of nymphomania."

"I'm not positive it's a euphemism."

"Be that as it may. And that led him to Gregory Vandiver's infirmity of purpose. Vandiver made some substantial investments in rare coins about a year ago. He consulted Bell, and purchased the pieces through Bell and on Bell's recommendation. He specifically sought out items for long-term growth, the blue chips of the coin market. Barber proofs, Charlotte and Dahlonega gold, that sort of thing. Then a matter of months ago, Vandiver insisted that Bell unload everything and get him cash overnight. It seems Vandiver did realize a profit on his investment, if a tiny one, but that Bell would have advised him to hold indefinitely, and certainly to hold for

103

several months, as an upturn could be expected in the market. But Vandiver insisted on selling immediately, even if he had to take a loss."

"Meaning that he needed cash, I guess."

"So it would seem. The money involved was considerable. I had to pry this from Bell, who evidently believes that matters communicated to a professional numismatist come under the category of privileged information. Gregory Vandiver liquidated his numismatic holdings for a net sum of $110,000."

"He had that much invested in coins?"

"I find that remarkable. I find it more remarkable that he had a sudden need for that much cash."

I nodded. "I wonder," I said.

"If he could have placed the bomb in the car?"

"Yeah. I suppose it's possible. Say he gets a train earlier than his usual one. He comes straight home and goes straight to the garage and wires the bomb to the Mercedes. He knows he's safe because he's not going to drive the car. He doesn't even think about Seamus because Caitlin usually drives herself." I stopped for a moment. "No, it doesn't add up. He wouldn't know she was going to use the car then. He didn't know I was there, so there was no way to know she would drive me home."

"He would assume she would use the car eventually, however."

"But why bother getting home earlier than usual? He could have planted the bomb some other time."

Haig leaned back and played with his beard. I asked a few more questions that he didn't respond to. I went over and watched the African gouramis· while he did his genius-in-residence number. While I was watching them, I saw the female knock off a guppy. It didn't bother me a bit.

Haig said, "I would like to know at what time Gregory Vandiver left his office."

"So would I."

"I would also like to know where Gordon McLeod spent the afternoon. And his source of income."

"So would I."

"There are other things, too. Several extremely curious

things. I am going to have to know considerably more about Cyrus Trelawney."

"I don't get it."

"Hmmmm," he said.

Wong brought us some beer and we sat opposite each other drinking it and arguing about where I was going to spend the night. "There is a pattern to all of this, Chip," he told me. "There are going to be more deaths. One develops the ability to sense this sort of thing. There have been four deaths already since the case engaged our interest. Melanie's was the first. The other three have been gratuitous. The prostitute, the sailor, the chauffeur."

"Manservant," I said.

"When a manservant dies at the wheel of his employer's car I have difficulty in not regarding him as a chauffeur. Three gratuitous deaths. There will be more deaths, and they will be more to the point. I sense this."

I went through my usual mental hassle as to whether he was a genius or a nut case.

"I would prefer that these deaths not occur. I will, in fact, endeavor to prevent them to the best of my ability. It is for this, after all, that I am employed. But, failing that, I would at least prefer that one of these deaths not be suffered by you."

"I'd prefer it, too." I said. "To tell you the truth."

"You expose yourself unnecessarily by returning to your rooming house."

"I expose myself to worse than that on the couch. I could die of a backache."

"You could have my bed," Haig said.

"Oh, don't be ridiculous."

"I would not mind the couch."

"Oh, come on. I'll walk a couple of blocks and I'll be home, for Pete's sake. It's nothing to worry about."

So I headed back to my rooming house.

That was my first mistake.

My second mistake happened as I was on my way up the steps

to the front door. A guy came out of the doorway to the left of my building, and two other guys came out of the doorway to the right of my building, and one of them asked me if I was Harrison, and I made my second mistake. I said I was.

13

THEY KICKED THE SHIT OUT OF ME.

14

I'M GOING TO LEAVE IT AT THAT.

Haig doesn't think I ought to. He wants me to handle it like Dick Francis and describe the beating they gave me, a blow at a time. With the proper discipline, he maintains, I can run the scene to ten or twelve pages instead of getting it over and done with in seven words. The thing is, I don't want to spend that much time remembering it. They kicked the shit out of me, very coldly and systematically, doing everything to assure me that there was nothing personal in what they were doing. Then they walked off in different directions, and I crawled into my rooming house and upstairs and got into bed.

Everything was worse in the morning. Things really ached. I dragged myself over to Haig's office and he took one look at me and threw a fit. What infuriated him the most was that I hadn't called him immediately so that he could have had his doctor look at me. I said I was pretty sure nothing was broken. He called his doctor, who made a housecall, which I felt was completely unnecessary. I think he came over for an excuse to look at the fish. But while he was there he also looked at me and pronounced me physically fit. I had a lot of bruises, and they were going to look increasingly ugly for the next week to ten days, but I had no broken bones and there was no evidence of internal injuries.

"You should have stayed here last night," Haig said.

I suppose he couldn't resist saying that. I didn't bother replying to it.

I had things to do, but they started with Kim and I couldn't see her until after noon when the hulk would either go to the docks or pretend to. I called Andrea Sugar, but failed to reach her. So I helped Haig with the fish until Wong brought us some

108

lunch. I can't remember what it was, only that it had slivers of almonds in it and it was delicious. Afterward Haig picked up the phone and called Addison Shivers' office. The old lawyer was in conference, but would return his call.

When Haig hung up I got through to Kim. "Gordie left a few minutes ago," she said. "Chip, maybe you shouldn't come over here. Gordie scares me a little."

He scared me more than a little, but I kept this fact to myself. "There was another murder attempt yesterday," I told her. "I'm on my way over."

This peeved Haig. "Mr. Shivers will be calling me shortly," he said. "You ought to be here when he does."

"I thought you wanted to talk to him yourself."

He leaned back in his chair and folded his hands on his stomach. "I do," he said. "But you should be present. I have a strong feeling that he is going to provide me with the solution to the case."

"Just like that?"

"Let us say he is going to give me evidence to support the conclusion I have drawn already."

"Conclusion?"

"On the basis of evidence already available to us."

"Evidence?"

"You're beginning to sound like an echo, Chip. Try to curb that tendency."

"I'll do my best. What evidence do we have already available to us? We have to find where Gordie spent yesterday afternoon and where he's been getting his money; we have to find out when Gregory Vandiver left his office and how deep a financial hole he's in, we have to—"

He waved a small hand at me. The right one, probably.

"Superficial," he said.

"But we don't know anything. Unless you've found out something and haven't told me."

"You have all the information I have."

"Do you want to tell me what I missed?"

"That would be premature," he said. He was disgustingly pleased with himself. "If you wait for Mr. Shivers' call—"

I decided he was grandstanding and I also decided I had better things to do than sit around waiting for the phone to ring. I sprung for a cab and rode down to Kim's place on Bethune Street. When she opened the door, the first thing I did was give her hell for not making sure it was me before unlocking the door.

"Then I'm in real danger," she said.

"You'd have to call it that. I was out on Long Island yesterday. To see Caitlin. Somebody wired a bomb to her car."

"Oh, God! She's not—"

"She's all right. But her chauffeur isn't. He was killed. It's pretty unmistakable, Kim. Somebody wants to kill every last one of you."

I got her to sit down and made her a cup of coffee. I sat on the couch next to her and patted her hand a lot and tried to be reassuring, which was tough because I had started off trying to scare her silly. I went on patting her hand, though, because I was beginning to enjoy it.

"I don't know what to do," she said.

Her eyes were wide with fear and innocence, and she was just so damned beautiful I wanted to kiss her. Instead I said, "Look, there are a lot of possibilities. One possibility is that you're not in any real danger at all. For the time being."

"I don't understand."

"Depending on who the killer is."

She thought that over, and then her face tightened. "You mean if I'm the one. I suppose you have to suspect everyone—"

"That's not what I meant at all, for Pete's sake. Look, I have to ask you this. Where was Gordie yesterday afternoon?"

"He was at work."

"The hell he was. Mr. Haig knows somebody who can ask questions on the docks and get the right answers. Gordie didn't show up for the shape-up yesterday. He didn't work at all."

She looked at me.

"He told you he worked from noon to eight?"

"Yes. Where was he if he wasn't at work?"

"That's what I'd like to find out. It also seems he's been losing big sums of money betting on slow horses. He's been losing more than he's been earning and I'd like to know where

110

he's been getting his money. Have you been giving him any?" I took her hand. "I know it's an embarrassing question, but I have to ask it."

"I don't mind. Because I've never given him anything. He's even tried to pay a share of the rent, but I haven't let him. He always takes the check when we go out together. He always seems to have plenty of money. A longshoreman can make a decent living and I thought—" She stopped suddenly.

"What's the matter?"

"I'm a slow study today, aren't I? You think he's been murdering my sisters."

"I think it's possible, yes. It's not the only possibility, but it's reasonably strong."

"It's so hard to believe."

"Could he have killed Melanie? That was Wednesday, sometime during the afternoon."

"He was working then. At least he told me so."

"And yesterday he had plenty of time to get out to Long Island and back. We'll have to find out if he has an alibi for Jessica's murder. I don't think he tracked Robin upstate and sabotaged her car. That sounds a little tricky. I think her death was accidental after all, but maybe it gave him the idea for the whole thing."

"How do you mean?"

"He must have figured that you would benefit financially by Robin's death. You don't, the money all goes to her husband, but he wouldn't necessarily know that. So he could have decided that if he killed off Jessica and Melanie and Caitlin you would have that much more money for him to marry."

She nodded with understanding. "So that's why I'm safe for the time being."

"Until you marry him and make out a will in his favor. That's if he's the killer. There are other possibilities."

"Who else do you suspect?"

"I don't want to mention any names yet. I wouldn't have said I suspected Gordie if there had been any other way to ask the questions I had to ask."

She went to make herself another cup of coffee and asked me if I wanted one. I said I wouldn't mind a beer. She brought one

111

and poured it into a glass for me. She didn't crumple the can when it was empty.

"I don't know how I'm going to behave in front of him," she said thoughtfully. "Just being aware that he might be a murderer is going to make it difficult for me."

"You can't let him know that you suspect. He wouldn't want to murder you ahead of schedule, but if it's a choice of doing that or being caught for the murders he's already committed—"

"It's going to be hard not to let anything show."

"Well, you'll get a chance to find out how good an actress you are."

"I will, won't I?" She set her coffee cup down and folded her hands on her knee. "I could believe that he might become violent. He's that type of person, there's a real potential for violence there. But I can't see him doing it in a calculated manner, if you know what I mean."

"That's bothered me from the start."

"Well, I'll be very careful."

"You'd better. That means two things, you know. Being careful not to let Gordie know you suspect him, and being careful not to be alone with anybody else. Don't open your door when you're here alone."

"For strangers, you mean."

"Or for people you know."

"God," she said. "You mean I have to suspect everybody, is that it?"

"Just about."

"It's been hard enough living with Gordie lately. And now to have this on my mind—"

I said, "Look, it's not my place to say this, but I'll say it anyway. I agree it's hard to imagine Gordie involved in such a complicated series of murders. It's also hard to imagine him involved with you. I mean, I really can't figure out what you see in a baboon like him."

She picked up her coffee cup and looked into it for a long time. Then without raising her eyes she said, "Oh, I don't know exactly. I haven't had much experience with men. Before

112

I met Gordie I fell in love with one of the boys in my acting class. He was a completely different type from Gordie. Very gentle and sensitive."

"I have a feeling I know how this ends."

"Of course. He turned out to be gay, which was something I probably should have recognized in the first place. The signs were all there. And it wasn't as though he did anything to encourage me to fall in love with him. He thought I knew what he was and just wanted to be friends." She looked up. "I took all of this terribly hard. And I decided that my next man was going to be as heterosexual as possible. Gordie was such a change, he had all this *macho* strength, and at the time I thought it was what I wanted."

"I gather you've changed your mind since."

"I know I couldn't marry him. Or even live with him much longer. Last night after your phone call I was furious with him. He had no right to act that way. I wanted to tell him to leave."

"What stopped you?"

"I think maybe I'm a little afraid of him. That he would take a punch at me or something." She managed a lopsided grin. "I'm a lot more afraid of him now than I was last night. After what you told me."

"Well, don't act any differently for the time being."

"I'll try not to. I can be a pretty good little actress when I have to."

"And an ornament to the stage. I think we'll crack the case in the next couple of days. And when all this is over—"

I left the sentence unfinished. I also left Kim's apartment after a few minutes because otherwise I might have found myself talking about what would happen when all this was over. I couldn't keep from having thoughts on the subject, but it was pretty silly to voice them at that stage. Premature, Haig would have called it.

I tried Andrea again. "I feel like a secret agent," she said. "I hoff zee documents."

"That's the worst Peter Lorre impression I ever heard, but it's good news. Can I come over?"

She gave me the address.

113

15

SHE LIVED IN THE SAME BUILDING she had occupied as Jessica's roommate. Not in the penthouse, however, but in a studio apartment on the third floor. She opened the door for me and motioned me inside. "Excuse the place," she said. "I haven't had time to buy any furniture that I like. That chair's not too bad."

As I was on my way to the chair that wasn't too bad she asked me if my leg was bothering me.

"Everything's bothering me," I said.

"I mean the way you walk. Did you hurt yourself?"

"I didn't have to. Someone did it for me."

"Huh?"

"I was beaten up last night. By professionals, I think. They didn't break any bones or anything like that. They just beat me to a pulp."

"Oh, God. Take your shirt off."

"Huh?"

"Take your shirt off and let me see. Christ, they really did a job on you. You're going to be stiff. Get undressed, Chip."

"Huh?"

"Take your clothes off and lie down on my bed. I'm serious, dumbbell. The only thing that's going to do you any good at this point is a massage. You should get a daily massage for the next week, as a matter of fact. Well, you came to the right place. I happen to be a damned good masseuse."

"I remember."

"Most of the girls don't know anything about muscle groups. I took the trouble to take a decent course. Come on, lie down on your stomach. Oh, you poor baby. They really worked you over, didn't they?"

"Ouch."

114

"Your flesh is very tender and I'll have to hurt you a little, but you'll feel a lot better afterward. Just trust me and try to relax."

"Okay."

She really knew what she was doing. She hurt me a little from time to time, but I could feel a lot of soreness and tension draining away. I began to feel very drowsy, and she had stopped touching me for a while before I realized the absence of her hands.

I asked if we were finished.

"Nope," she said cheerfully. "I'm taking my clothes off. I work better in the nude. Okay, tiger. Roll over."

I rolled over and opened my eyes. That long lean body was even nicer than I remembered it.

I said, "I don't know about this."

"You don't have to," she said. "Just shut up and relax. Does this hurt?"

"Yes."

"Those rotten bastards. There, that's better, isn't it?"

I was beginning to feel a little stirring. You probably don't find that hard to believe. Her hands were very firm and very gentle, and her body was very beautiful, and she had that nice spicy smell to her skin. When she started touching my thighs with that feathery way she had, I started to sit up. She made me lie down again.

"Hey," I said.

"Feels nice, doesn't it?"

"Yeah, but I really don't want to wind up frustrated."

"That must have been awful the other day. I hated to see you leave like that."

"I didn't like it much myself, but I don't have any money now and I—"

"Who said anything about money, Chip?"

"Huh?"

She grinned wickedly. "Dumbbell. I'm not working now, you jerk. I'm on my own time, and I'm giving you a massage because you can use one. This is just therapy for you, baby. I'm not going to leave you tied up in knots. I'm going to untie knots you never knew you had."

"Oh."

"Now you lie still and just enjoy this. I'm going to take my time, and it may seem as though I'm teasing you, but it'll just make it that much better at the end. You're going to love this, baby."

She used her hands and her breasts and her lips and tongue. She found erogenous zones I hadn't known I had, and at times it did seem as though she was teasing me, and at times I thought I would die if it didn't end soon, and at times I wanted it to go on forever, and at the very end she turned her sweet mouth into a vacuum cleaner and turned me inside-out.

"Jesus," I said.

"I told you you were gonna love it."

"You're absolutely fantastic."

"Well, I do this for a living, honey. There's a lot to be said for professionalism."

"I guess there is."

"If I weren't reasonably competent by now, I'd go into some other line of work. But I don't get many complaints."

"You won't get one from me."

"Come on," she said, slapping me lightly on the thigh. "Put some clothes on and I'll show you what I stole for you. And where do you get off saying I do a lousy impression of Peter Lorre? That wasn't Peter Lorre. That was Akim Tamiroff, and I do a great Akim Tamiroff."

There was quite a stack of membership application forms from the two-week period preceding Jessica's death. Indulgence evidently did a hell of a business, and if all its recreational therapists were like Andrea, I could understand why.

What I couldn't understand at first was why I was bothering to go through this pile of paper, since every third person seemed to be named John Smith. And most of the others were pretty obvious aliases. I read in one of Haig's books that amateurs almost always use a first name, or a form of one, as the last name of their alias. So I ran into a high percentage of names like John Richards, Joe Andrews, Sam Joseph, and so on.

116

Then I hit a name I knew, and then I hit it again, and then I hit it a third time, and I cabbed to Haig's house with three pieces of paper in my pocket that would wrap up a murderer.

16

HE WAS AT HIS DESK. "You left just before Mr. Shivers called me," he said. He looked intolerably smug. "You'll perhaps be pleased to know that my instincts were quite on the mark. I thought I knew who the killer was, and now all doubt has been removed."

"So has mine."

"Oh? That's interesting. I'd enjoy hearing the line of reasoning you followed."

"I didn't follow any line of reasoning," I said. "My legwork evidently got to the same place as your brainwork, and at about the same time. I reached Andrea Sugar and checked the records of men who had been to Indulgence shortly before Jessica was killed. I didn't expect anything to come of it because I didn't figure he would use his right name, but he probably had to because Jessica would recognize him."

"That's logical."

"Thank you. He didn't just go there once. He went there three times within the week preceding her death. I was thinking that you could call that a lot of nerve, but one thing the guy has not lacked is nerve. He's about the nerviest bastard I've ever heard of."

"That's well put."

"Thank you."

"You are welcome." His hand went to his beard. "I find it fascinating the way your legwork and my mental work found the same goal by opposite routes. Do you remember something I told you the other day? That there was a definite Ross MacDonald cast to this entire affair?"

"Something about forty years ago in Canada."

"That's correct. But it's closer to fifty years than forty, and the locale is somewhat south of the Canadian border." He closed his eyes and stroked his beard some more. "What an extraordinary amount of planning he devoted to all of this. The man has elements of genius. He's also quite mad, of course. The combination is by no means unheard of."

"Well, we've got him now. And these three slips of paper nail him to the wall."

And I passed them across to Haig.

"Gregory Vandiver," he read aloud.

"May he rot in hell."

"But this is very curious," he said.

"What's curious about it? I already explained why he must have figured he had to use his right name. Because Jessica would have known him already. You told me I was logical."

"I never said you were logical. I said that particular statement was logical."

"Well, what's the problem? Vandiver has had cash problems. Of all the people in the case, he's the only one with a real money motive. For most people the difference between two million dollars and ten million dollars doesn't matter much, but he got into investments over his head and needed the prospect of really big money. So he—"

"Be quiet, Chip."

"Oh, for Pete's sake—"

"Chip. Be quiet."

I became quiet. He turned around and watched the rasboras for a while. They ignored him and I tried to. He turned to face me, but his eyes were closed and he was playing with his beard. Sometime I'm going to shave him in his sleep, and he'll never be able to think straight again.

He had been wearing his beard away for maybe five minutes when the doorbell rang. I stayed where I was and let Wong get it. A few seconds later he brought in a man who looked familiar. It took me a second or two to place him as one of the Sands Point police officers.

He said, "Mr. Harrison? I'm Luther Polk, we met yesterday afternoon."

"Yes," I said. I introduced him to Haig, who had by now opened his eyes. "I suppose you want a further statement, but I don't think—"

119

"No, it's not that," he said. "I will need a further statement from you eventually, but there's something else. Do you want to sit down?"

"No, but if you'd be more comfortable—"

He shook his head. "I have some bad news for you," he said slowly. "I felt I ought to bring it in person. Late last night or early this morning Mrs. Vandiver shot and killed her husband. She then took her own life. The bodies were discovered by servants at approximately ten this morning. Mrs. Vandiver left a sealed envelope addressed to you beside her typewriter. Under the circumstances it was necessary to open and read the letter. It's a suicide note, and explains the reasons for her actions. I thought you would like to have it. I'll need to retain it as evidence, but you may examine it now if you wish."

This is the note:

Dear Chip,

By the time you read this I will probably be dead by my own hand. Unless I lose my nerve, and I might. But I don't think so.

It was Gregory who tried to kill me by planting a bomb in my car. It was also Gregory who killed Melanie and Jessica and Robin, and he would have killed Kim too in due time. I found this out an hour ago when he tried a second time to kill me. He was attempting to strangle me in my sleep. I woke up in time to get loose. I've always kept a small pistol in my bedside table. I managed to get it in time. I shot him and killed him. In a few minutes I think I'll shoot myself.

I'm just so tired, Chip. Tired of everything. It's astonishing that I could have been married to this man for so long without sensing his evil nature. I merely took it for granted that he was a bore. I never had an inkling that he was a homicidal maniac into the bargain.

Maybe I'm in shock. Maybe suicide is an irrational act for me to perform. I certainly don't feel guilty for having killed Gregory. It was self-defense, certainly, and I would be let off for that reason. So maybe I'm just using this as an excuse for something I've wanted to do for a long time.

120

I don't know if you can understand this, since I scarcely understand it myself. But I somehow think you might be able to, Chip.

Please don't think too badly of me.

I read it through a couple of times. Then I gave it to Haig. "She was my client," he said, "and I failed to protect her."

Luther Polk said, "Sir, if she was determined to take her own life—"

"If I had had one more day," Haig said. "one more day."

"It was definitely self-defense, just as she wrote it," Polk went on. "There were abrasions on her throat from where her husband had tried to strangle her, and—"

"Pfui!" Haig said. "Caitlin Vandiver did not write this bit of fiction. Gregory Vandiver did not attempt to strangle her. She did not shoot him. She did not shoot herself."

Polk just stared down at him.

"A little over forty years ago," Haig said. "And a bit to the south of Canada."

I probably should have picked up on it by then, but I was only half hearing the words. I picked up one of the membership forms from the desk and looked at the signature, and then I got it.

"Oh," I said.

Haig looked at me.

"I just recognized the handwriting," I told him. "But what I can't figure out is why. I know, forty years ago in Canada. But why?"

"In a quick phrase?" He touched his beard. "Because he didn't have the guts to kill his father," he said.

I tried to make some sense out of that one while Haig began listing names on a memorandum slip. Polk was saying something in the background. He must have felt as though he had walked into a Pinter play after having missed the first act. We both ignored him. Haig finished making his list and handed it to me.

"I want these people in this room in an hour's time. Do what you have to do to arrange it."

I read half the list and looked at him. "Oh, for Pete's sake," I said. "You're not really going to do a whole production number, are you? Everybody in one room together while you show them what a genius you are. I mean, all you have to do is call the police."

"Chip." He folded his hands on his desk. "This is the most extraordinary case I have ever had. The criminal is an archfiend of terrifying proportions. I am going to play this one strictly according to the book."

17

YOU WOULDN'T BELIEVE WHAT I went through, getting them all there. And I couldn't possibly bring it off in an hour, even with Luther Polk on hand to expedite matters. Polk was helpful, especially once he came to the conclusion that he was not going to know anything about what was going on until Leo Haig was ready to tell him.

"He's a genius," I explained. "He was telling me just a few hours ago that there's a very thin line between genius and insanity. You can think of him as walking along that line, doing a high-wire act on it."

"But you say he's about to come up with a killer."

"He's going to come down on one," I said. "With both feet. And he's got enough weight to land hard."

"Not all that much weight," Polk said. "He'd be right trim if you was to stretch him out to a suitable length."

I pushed the image of Leo Haig being lengthened on a medieval rack as far out of mind as possible, and settled down to the serious business of setting the stage and assembling the audience. It took two hours and twelve minutes, and I think that was pretty good.

They arrived in stages, of course, but I won't burden you with the order of their coming, or the way I fielded their questions and settled them down. I'll just tell you what the room looked like when Haig condescended to enter it.

Wong Fat and I had set up a double row of chairs on my side of the partners' desk, facing Haig. My own chair was off to the side, between the audience and the door.

In the front row, farthest from me, sat Detective Vincent Gregorio. He was wearing a black silk suit with a subtle dark blue stripe and a pair of wing tip loafers you could see your face in if you were in a house where they covered the mirrors. I don't

123

know where he bought his clothes, but between them and his twenty-dollar haircut he looked like a walking advertisement for police corruption. I was surprised that he had agreed to come so readily. Maybe he got a charge out of it when Haig called him a witling.

Andrea Sugar sat on Gregorio's right, which was an obvious source of pleasure to Kid Handsome, because he was doing a courtship dance that a male *Betta splendens* would have been proud of, preening and posing and not knowing how little good it was going to do him. Andrea was wearing a maroon dress with bright red cherries all over it, and if you can't think of the thoughts it inspired, that's too damned bad, because I am not going to spell them out for you.

I had put Addison Shivers, our sole surviving client, alongside Andrea. That also put him directly across the desk from Haig, which seemed only proper. He was the angel for this theatrical production. His suit was probably as old as detective Gregorio, but it still looked good. He sat quite stiff in his chair, and when Haig came into the room he took off his glasses and cleaned them with his necktie.

Kim was seated next to Mr. Shivers, with Gordie McLeod on the other side of her, which put him in the chair closest to mine. This had not been my idea. I would have preferred to be able to look directly at Kim without having him around to play the role of an automobile graveyard at the foot of a beautiful mountain. That's a bad choice of words, actually, because Kim could not have looked less mountainous. She seemed to have grown smaller and more petite in the short time since I had seen her. She was wearing what she had worn earlier. I had seen nothing to object to then and I saw nothing to object to now, except for the hulking moron who was holding her hand in his paw.

McLeod was wearing something loutish. I think he'd put on a clean bowling shirt in honor of the occasion. His shoes needed a shine and probably weren't going to get one. They had thick soles, for stepping on people.

Detective Wallace Seidenwall was directly behind McLeod, which put him closer to me than I might have wanted him. He had not grown discernibly fonder of me since our last meeting. "This better be good," was a phrase which came trippingly to his lips during the waiting period. He didn't say it as though he thought it was going to, either. He was wearing a gray glen plaid suit that Robert Hall had marked down for good reason. Either his partner got all the graft, or Seidenwall was running a yacht, or something, because he was due for a bitter disappointment again this fall when the Best Dressed list came out.

Ferdinand Bell was next to Seidenwall, and he was the only one in the crowd who looked genuinely happy to be present. "This will be a treat," he said upon entering, and he enjoyed himself immensely making small talk with the others and asking the names of all of the fish. He had on the same suit he'd worn to Melanie's funeral. His short white hair set off his pink scalp, or maybe it was the other way around, and his plump cheeks reminded you more than ever of a chipmunk when he smiled, which was most of the time.

I had stuck Luther Polk next to Bell, which put him directly behind Addison Shivers. (I know I'm taking forever giving you the geography of all this, and I know you could probably care less about the whole thing, but Haig spent so much time charting it out that it is conceivably important. I know I'd catch hell if I didn't go through it all.) I don't think I described Polk before, but if you've seen Dennis Weaver in that television series where he plays an Arizona marshal attached to the New York Police Department, then I won't have to describe him for you. He had had relatively little to say to the two Homicide detectives, or they to him, and he sat there keeping his hand comfortingly close to the revolver on his hip.

Madam Juana was sitting on the far side of Polk. She was wearing her basic black dress and a string of pearls, and she looked like the stern-lipped administrator of a parochial school for girls. (I can't help it, that's what she looked like.)

Well, it wasn't what you would call perfect. I mean, there should have been three or four more obvious suspects present. John LiCastro would have been a nice addition to the group, but Haig had pointed out that it would have been an insensitive

125

act to place him in the same room with policemen for no compelling reason. And it would have been even nicer if our other client had been present; if Haig had had just a few more hours to work with, Caitlin would have been alive.

So it wasn't perfect, but it was still a pretty decent showing, and I have to admit I got a kick out of it when Leo Haig marched into the room and every eye turned to take in the sight of him.

He seated himself very carefully behind his desk. I had a bad moment when I thought he was going to put his feet up, but he got control of himself. He took his time meeting the eyes of each person in the room, including me, and then he closed his eyes and touched his beard and went into a tiny huddle with himself. It didn't last as long as it might have.

He opened his eyes and said, "I want to thank you for coming here. I am going to unmask a killer this afternoon, a killer who has in one way or another affected all our lives. Each of us has been thus affected, but not all of you are aware of the extent of this killer's activities. So you must permit me to rehash some recent events. Not all of them will be news to any of you, and one of you will know all of what I am about to say, and more. Because the murderer is in this room."

He was grandstanding, but of course it went over well. Everybody turned and looked at everybody else.

"This past Wednesday," Haig said, "my associate Mr. Harrison discovered the body of Miss Melanie Trelawney. She had died of an overdose of heroin. Previously she had told Mr. Harrison that she feared for her life. His observations of the scene at Miss Trelawney's apartment led Mr. Harrison to the certain conclusion that she had been murdered. When he confided his observations to me—"

"Wait a minute," Gregorio cut in. "Where do you get off concealing evidence from the police?"

"I concealed no evidence," Haig said. "Nor did Mr. Harrison. Nothing was suppressed, nothing distorted. It is not incumbent upon a citizen to apprise the police of his suspicions. Indeed, it is often unwise.

"To continue. When Mr. Harrison confided his observations to me, I concurred in his conclusion. Miss Trelawney's fears were predicated, it appeared, upon the fact that two of her sisters had recently suffered violent deaths, one the apparent victim of suicide, the other the apparent victim of an automobile accident. I determined at once to ferret out the killer and prevent him from doing further damage. I have at least succeeded in the first attempt, if not in the second."

Gregorio broke in again. "I'd like to know what made you think that OD was murder," he said. "If we missed something, I'd like to know what it was."

"In due time, sir. In due time. Permit me, if you will, to explore events chronologically. The day after Miss Trelawney's death, Mr. Harrison and I began a series of inquiries. In the course of so doing, we were engaged by Mr. Addison Shivers to look after the best interests of Cyrus Trelawney, deceased. It is perhaps unusual for an attorney to engage detectives for the benefit of a client who is no longer living. In my eyes, Mr. Shivers' act stands greatly to his credit."

The hand went to the beard again. I looked around the room and watched everybody watching Haig. Gordie McLeod looked as though he was trying to understand the big words. Juana looked as though she was trying to understand the English words. Kim looked as though she was trying to figure out how Haig could hold an audience in the palm of his hand, just by sitting there with his eyes closed while he played with his facial hair.

"On the following day Mr. Harrison attended Miss Trelawney's funeral, both to pay his respects to the deceased and to press our investigation. There he met Mrs. Gregory Vandiver, the former Caitlin Trelawney, who also engaged us to look into the matter of her sister's death. I accepted a retainer from her, feeling no conflict of interest was likely to be involved."

He paused to glance directly at Addison Shivers, who gave a barely perceptible nod.

"Mr. Harrison returned to this office. We were seated in this very room when a pipe bomb was thrown into the front room

127

a floor below. Several of my aquaria suffered minor damage. This was galling, but of little actual importance. Of major importance was the fact that the bombing caused two deaths. Maria Tijerino, an associate of Miss Juana Dominguez, and Elmer J. Seaton, a seaman on shore leave, were in the room into which the bomb was hurled. Both were killed instantly."

A couple of heads turned to look at Madam Juana, who crossed herself several times.

"Detectives Gregorio and Seidenwall, who investigated the bombing, assumed that the premises below were the bomber's target. The nature of the business carried on downstairs would tend to further such a suspicion. The world overflows with maniacs who feel they are doing the Creator's work by blowing brothels to smithereens. Mr. Harrison and I interpreted the bombing in a different fashion."

"I told you we oughta take him in," Seidenwall said. "What did I tell you? I told you we oughta take him in."

Haig ignored this. "My immediate thought was that the bomber had chosen the wrong window. It did not take me long to realize that I was in error. A person anxious to kill me would do a better job of it, especially in view of his skill in arranging other murders. No, the bombing had been meant either to discourage me from further investigations, or to pique my interest in the case. I could not, at that stage, determine which.

"But the bombing did tell me certain things about the killer. It told me, first of all, that he knew I was on his trail. This did little to narrow the field of suspects. It told me, too, that the man I was dealing with was quite ruthless, willing to liquidate innocent strangers in order to advance his machinations. I was on the trail of a dangerous, desperate and wholly immoral human being."

Haig picked up a pipe, took it deliberately apart, ran a pipe cleaner unnecessarily through it and put it back together again.

"My investigations continued. Yesterday my associate visited Mrs. Vandiver at her home on Long Island. While he was there, a bomb wired to the automobile of Mrs. Vandiver was detonated, killing her chauffeur, one Seamus Fogarty. The local police officers assumed Mr. Fogarty was the intended

128

victim because of his political activities. I assumed otherwise. An attempt had been made on my client's life.

"Last night my associate, Mr. Harrison, left this house against my advice—" He had to rub it in, damn it. "—and returned to his own lodgings. He was set upon and badly beaten by three strangers, evidently professionals at that sort of thing." Eyes swung around to look at me. There was concern in Kim's, surprise in Ferdinand Bell's, and what looked annoyingly like satisfaction in Seidenwall's.

"And later last night," Haig went on, "or perhaps early this morning, the killer struck again. He murdered Mr. and Mrs. Gregory Vandiver and arranged things to suggest that Mrs. Vandiver shot her husband and then took her own life."

Kim let out a shriek, and the whole room began mumbling to itself. McLeod reached for her. She drew away. Haig tapped on the desk top with a pipe.

"I learned of this last act just a few hours ago. My first reaction was to feel personally responsible for the deaths of Mr. and Mrs. Vandiver. By the time I learned of their fate, I already knew the identity of their killer. I did not know, however, at the time they were killed. Perhaps I could still have done something, taken some action, to prevent what happened to them. I had held strong suspicions of the murderer's identity for some time."

He closed his eyes for a moment. I took a good long look at the killer, and did not obtain the slightest idea of what was going through his mind.

"Officer Polk brought me the news of what happened to my client and her husband. He also brought a typed and unsigned suicide note which the murderer had had the temerity to write. The note was designed to wrap up all of the crimes to date and pin them upon Gregory Vandiver, who was supposed to have attempted to kill his wife, was then killed by her, after which my client is supposed to have suffered an uncharacteristic fit of remorse at the conclusion of which she killed herself.

"There was no reason for Officer Polk to doubt this charade. I suspect his department might have doubted it ultimately. But Mr. Harrison and myself immediately recognized it as illusion,

129

and read in the purported suicide note additional confirmation of the identity of the actual killer."

Polk said, "How did you know so quickly the note was a fake?"

I fielded that one. "I knew it on the first line," I said. "The murderer spelled my first name right. C-h-i-p. Caitlin thought I spelled it with two p's; she made out a check that way. I never corrected her." I didn't add that I had suspected Greg Vandiver all along and it just about took the note to change my mind. Let them think I was as brilliant as Leo Haig.

"The concept of leaving a typewritten suicide note was a bad one," Haig added. "But the murderer had developed an extraordinary degree of gall. Success engenders confidence. Mr. Harrison has described the killer as the nerviest bastard he ever heard of. I told him that was exceedingly well put, as you will come to realize."

I watched the killer's face on that line. I think it got to him a little bit.

"The killer wanted to round things off neatly," Haig went on. "He knew better than to leave a note when he pushed Jessica Trelawney out of her window. Now, though, he wanted to establish Gregory Vandiver as the villain of the piece, and award him a posthumous citation for multiple homicide. At this very moment he may be cursing himself for his stupidity. He might better save himself the effort. I already knew him as the killer. This was by no means his first witless act. But it is to be his last."

Haig closed his eyes again. I can't speak for the rest of the company, but for me the tension was getting unbearable. I knew something the rest of them didn't know, and I wished he would hurry up and get to the end.

"This morning I called Mr. Shivers. In addition to being my client, he was for a great many years both attorney and friend to the late Cyrus Trelawney. He was able to supply me with the last piece of my jigsaw puzzle, the question of motive.

"I had realized almost from the beginning that motive was the key element of these murders. The most immediately obvious motive was money. The case is awash with money.

130

Cyrus Trelawney left a fortune in excess of ten million dollars. But the more I examined the facts, the less likely it seemed that money could constitute a motive.

"Why, then, would someone want to murder five women who had virtually nothing in common but their kinship? Several possibilities presented themselves. The first was that, having determined to murder one of them for a logical reason, he might have wished to disguise his act by making it one link in a chain of homicides. Gregory Vandiver, for example, could have had reason to do away with his wife. If he first killed some of her sisters, he would be a less obvious suspect for the single murder for which he had a visible motive.

"The fault in this line of reasoning is not difficult to pinpoint. If a person wished to create the appearance of a chain of murders, he would make the façade an unmistakable one. He would not disguise his handiwork as accidental death or suicide. He would make each act an obvious murder, and would probably use the same murder method in each instance. So this was not a *faked* chain of murders, but a very *real* chain of murders.

"And then I saw that the answer had to lie in the past. These girls were being killed because they were the daughters of Cyrus Trelawney. The man had died three years ago, and after his death his daughters began dying. First Robin, then Jessica, then Melanie. And now Caitlin."

He did start to put his feet up then, I'm positive of it, but he caught himself in time.

"I've told Mr. Harrison that this case reminded me of the work of a certain author of detective stories. Our New York has little of the texture of Lew Archer's California, but in much the same way the sins of the past work upon those of us trapped in the present. If I were to find the killer, I had to consider Cyrus Trelawney.

"Cyrus Trelawney." He folded his hands on the desk top. "An interesting man, I should say. Fathered his first child at the age of forty-eight, having beforehand amassed a fortune. Continued fathering them every three years, spawning as regularly as a guppy. Brought five girls into the world. And one

131

son who died in his cradle. I began to wonder about Cyrus Trelawney's life before he married. I speculated, and I constructed an hypothesis."

He paused and looked across his desk at Addison Shivers. "This morning I asked Mr. Shivers a question. Do you recall the question, sir?"

"I do."

"Indeed. Would you repeat it?"

"You asked if Cyrus Trelawney had been a man of celibate habits before his marriage."

"And your reply?"

"That he had not."

(This was paraphrase. What Mr. Shivers had actually said, Haig told me later, was that Cyrus Trelawney would fuck a coral snake if anybody would hold its head.)

"I then asked Mr. Shivers several other questions which elicited responses I had expected to elicit. I learned, in brief, that Mr. Trelawney's business interests forty-five to fifty years ago included substantial holdings in timberlands and paper mills in upstate New York. That he spent considerable time in that area during those years. That one of those mills was located in the town of Lyons Falls, New York."

"That's very interesting," the killer said.

"Indeed. But the others do not understand what makes it interesting, Mr. Bell. Would you care to tell them?"

"I was born in Lyons Falls," Bell said.

"Indeed. You were born in Lyons Falls, New York, forty-seven years ago last April 18th. Your mother was a woman named Barbara Hohlbein who was the wife of a man named James Bell. James Bell was not your father. Cyrus Trelawney was your father. Cyrus Trelawney's daughters were your half-sisters and you have killed four of the five, Mr. Bell, and you will not kill any more of them. You will not, Mr. Bell. No, sir. You will not."

18

OF COURSE EVERYBODY STARED AT the son of a bitch. He didn't seem to notice. His eyes were on Leo Haig and he was as cool as a gherkin. His forehead looked a little pinker, but that may have been my imagination. I couldn't really tell you.

"This is quite fascinating," Bell said. "I asked around when I heard you were investigating Melanie's death. I was told that you were quite insane. I wondered what this elaborate charade would lead to."

"I would prefer that it lead to the gas chamber, sir. I fear it will lead only to permanent incarceration in a hospital for the criminally insane."

"Fascinating."

"Indeed. I shouldn't attempt to leave if I were you, Mr. Bell. There are police officers seated on either side of you. They would take umbrage."

"Oh, I wouldn't miss this for the world," Bell said. His cheeks puffed out as he grinned. "Why, if this were a movie I'd *pay* to see it. It's *far* more thrilling in real life."

Haig closed his eyes. Without opening them he said, "I have no way of knowing whether or not Cyrus Trelawney was your father. You do not resemble him, nor do I perceive any resemblance between yourself and his legitimate offspring. Very strong men tend to be prepotent, which is to say that their genes are dominant. Much the same is true of fishes, you might be interested to know. I would guess that you resemble your mother. I suspect you inherited your madness from her."

A muscle worked in Bell's temple. He didn't say anything.

"I don't doubt that she told you Trelawney was your father. I don't doubt that you believe it, that you grew up hearing little more from her than that a rich man had fathered you. It certainly made an impression upon you. You grew up loving

133

and hating this man you had never met. You were obsessed by the idea that he had sired you. Had he acknowledged you, you would have been rich. Money became an obsession.

"One learns much about a man from his hobbies. You collect money, Mr. Bell. Not in an attempt to amass wealth, but as a way of playing with the symbols of wealth. Little pieces of stamped metal moving from hand to hand at exorbitant prices. Pfui!"

"Numismatics is a science."

"Anything may be taken for a science when enough of its devotees attempt to codify their madness. There is a young man in this city, I understand, who spends his spare time, of which I trust he has an abundance, analyzing the garbage of persons understandably more prominent than himself. For the time being he is acknowledged to be a lunatic. If, heaven forfend, his pastime amasses a following, garbage analysis will be esteemed a science. Learned books will be published on the subject. Fools will write them. Greater fools will purchase and read them. Pfui!"

"You know nothing about numismatics," Bell said.

Haig grunted. "I could dispute that. I shall not take the trouble. I am not concerned with numismatics, sir. I am concerned with murder."

"And you're calling me a murderer."

"I have done so already." He stroked his beard briefly. "I've no idea just when you planned to become a murderer. At your mother's knee, I would suppose. You came to New York. You established yourself in your profession. You kept tabs on your father. And, because of your infirmity of purpose, you bided your time.

"Because you could not kill this man, nor could you think of relinquishing the dream of killing him. You waited until time achieved what you could not: the death of Cyrus Trelawney."

"And then I married Robin."

"Then you married Robin Trelawney," Haig agreed with him.

"And then I crashed up the car and killed her, I suppose. The only person I ever loved and I crashed up my car on the chance that I would live through the wreck and she would not."

134

"No, sir. No in every respect. But I'll back up a bit. Before you married Robin, indeed before Cyrus Trelawney died, you had all of your plan worked out. The first step called for you to murder Phillip Flanner."

"Now I *know* you're insane," Bell said.

"You told Mr. Harrison that you were a friend of Flanner's, that he was a fellow numismatist. He was not. You did become a friend of his, but not until after he and Robin were married. You ingratiated yourself with him because he had recently taken her as a wife."

"He fell in front of a subway car."

"You threw him in front of a subway car."

"You couldn't prove that in a million years."

"I haven't the slightest need to prove it. You are a very curious man, Mr. Bell. You took your time ingratiating yourself with Robin. You waited until her father was at last in his grave before you persuaded her to marry you. Then you waited a couple of years before you killed her. You must have thought about the murder method for all of that time and more."

"I loved Robin."

"No, sir. You have never loved anyone, except insofar as you loved Cyrus Trelawney. I leave that to the psychiatrists, who will have ample opportunity to inquire. You drove with Robin to a coin convention. At some time in the course of the ride back, you broke her neck. That would not have been terribly difficult to manage. Then you put her in the back of the car and found a place where an icy road surface could explain an accident. You then effected that accident, sir, which no doubt took a certain amount of insane courage on your part."

"No one will believe this."

"I suspect everyone in the room already believes it, sir. But they will not have to, nor will anyone else." Haig turned around and looked at the rasboras. I was astonished, and I was used to him, so you can imagine what it did to everybody else. But I'll be damned if anyone said a word. I was wondering how long he was going to milk it, when he turned around again and got to his feet.

"The order of the murders," he said. "Robin, Jessica,

135

Melanie, Caitlin. I was shocked when I learned that Caitlin was dead. Doubly shocked, because I thought you would save her for last. You were trying so hard to throw suspicion upon Gregory Vandiver. Inventing some nonsense about financial insolvency, some prattle about his having invested large sums in rare coins and being forced to liquidate them. One would have thought you would wait until Kim was safely dead before disposing of him. He, surely, would have done so before killing his wife, had he the financial motive you suggested.

"But that becomes clear when one devotes some thought to it. You did not merely want to murder your half-sisters. You wanted to have sexual relations with them as well.

"First Robin. You married her in order to have sex with her. Then Jessica. You went at least three times to her place of employment in the week preceding her death. You signed Gregory Vandiver's name to the membership application, having already planned to use him as a scapegoat should there be need for one. Through this contact with Jessica, you were able to arrange to see her privately at her apartment. You did so, sir, and you pitched her out of her window."

"You can't prove that," Bell said.

"But I can. Miss Sugar no doubt recognizes you. If not, her colleagues very possibly will. In any event, I have here three pieces of paper confirming the dates of your visits. They identify you as Gregory Vandiver, sir, but they are in your handwriting."

Which is how I had tipped to the whole thing. I remembered where I had seen that precise penmanship. It was on a 2 x 2 coin envelope.

"You had an affair with Caitlin. I have had it established that this was not terribly difficult for one to achieve. I knew at an early date that you were probably in touch with her. I learned that when Mr. Harrison reported on his conversation with you Saturday."

I said, "How?"

Haig glared at me.

"I'm serious. How did you know that?"

"Because you've learned to report conversations verbatim. I

spoke to Mr. Bell over the telephone to prepare him for your visit. I identified you as my associate, Mr. Harrison. I did not mention your first name. Nor did you mention it when introducing yourself. Mr. Bell asked if it was all right for him to call you Chip. The only person likely to have told him your name was Caitlin, yet he gave the impression that everything you were saying to him was coming as a great surprise. This made me instantly suspicious of Mr. Bell, a suspicion I never had cause to relinquish."

"I was not having an affair with Caitlin," Bell said stiffly. "As a matter of fact, she did ask my advice after Harrison talked to her. She had second thoughts about hiring him, and wanted my opinion."

"Indeed."

"I never had sexual relations with her. Or with Jessica. Perhaps it's true that I visited her at that massage parlor. If I signed Gregory's name, it was on a whim. I only visited her to have a half hour of her time, so that we could talk about Robin. It was a way of bringing Robin back to life for me."

Haig closed his eyes. He opened them and sighed and sat down behind his desk again. "I won't comment on that," he said. "Nor shall I attempt to determine what sexual act you performed with Melanie Trelawney. I suspect it might have been you who put the thought in her mind that her two sisters had been killed. Or you might have become aware of her suspicions by virtue of her having called you to inquire if there was any possibility that Robin's death was not wholly accidental. At any rate, it should have posed no problem for you to gain access to her apartment. Once there, you could have had little difficulty in rendering her unconscious. She was completely nude when Mr. Harrison discovered the body. It has not been my observation that people habitually disrobe before injecting themselves with heroin."

"Happens some of the time," Gregorio said.

"Sometimes, yes, sometimes no. You wouldn't get suspicious either way," Seidenwall said.

Haig nodded. " So you would not have disrobed her to make her the more obvious victim of death from a drug overdose. I'm sure you did something with her. I do not care to know what it was, nor do I care to know whether it took place before or after you injected a fatal overdose of the drug into her bloodstream."

I don't care to know that either, to tell you the truth.

"You can't prove any of this," Bell said. Not for the first time.

Haig stared at him. He was on his feet again. "I can prove almost all of it," he said. "Once the facts are known and established, the proof is rarely hard to come by. Had you taken your time, you might have managed to bring it off. You did come very close at that. You killed four out of five. Had sex with four of your sisters, killed four of your sisters.

"And you were very patient at the onset. You waited to kill Phillip Flanner, waited to marry his widow, waited to kill her. But then you got a taste of it and you liked it, didn't you? *You loved it.*"

Bell didn't say anything. The muscle was really having a workout in his temple, and he didn't look his usual happy self.

"You incestuous murdering bastard," Haig said. "You never did what you wanted to do. You never killed your father and you never slept with your mother, and you used your sisters as surrogates for both, one after another. But you'll never get the last one, Bell, you'll never put a hand on her!"

The son of a bitch moved fast. He had the knife out of his pocket and the blade open before I could even blink.

A fat lot of good it did him. He wasn't even out of his chair before Seidenwall had an arm wrapped around his throat and Luther Polk's long-barreled automatic was jabbed into the side of his head.

They took turns advising him of his rights. He went limp, but that didn't make Seidenwall let go of his throat or Polk stop jabbing him in the head with the gun barrel.

On the way out, his hands cuffed behind his back, he turned and smiled at me. It was a smile I will never forget as long as I live. I can close my eyes and see it now. I wish I couldn't.

"You know," he said, "I had absolutely nothing to do with having you beaten up. I hope you can believe that."

138

19

AFTER THE THREE COPS had escorted Ferdinand Bell out of
there, I figured everybody would start talking at once. I guess
nobody wanted to make the first move. They all just sat there
staring at each other.

Finally Addison Shivers said, "The vagaries and
inconsistencies of human nature. How many persons did that
man kill?"

"I know of nine," Haig said. "The four sisters; Phillip
Flanner; Maria Tijerina; Elmer Seaton, the sailor; Seamus
Fogarty; Gregory Vandiver. Nine. There may have been
others, but I doubt it."

"And yet the one crime he was anxious to deny was the
administration of a beating to young Chip."

"Indeed," Haig said. "He was not responsible for it, as it
happens."

Kim said, to me, "You never told me you were beaten up."

I agreed that I never did.

"If he didn't do it, then who did?"

I got to my feet. It was doomed to be anticlimactic, but it was
my part of the show. "That's easy to answer," I said. "Gordie
McLeod set me up. Didn't you, old buddy?"

Everybody stared at him. He didn't return the favor. He
stared at his hands, mostly. Kim got up and drew away from
him as if he was a leper. Which, come to think of it, he more
or less was.

I said. "Well?"

He stood up. "I made a mistake," he said.

I just looked at him.

"Well, I'll tell you, man. All I could see is you're nosin'
around my girl. And then I find out you've got some people
down to the docks askin' questions about me. What do I need

139

with people askin' questions, and I don't know about any murders, and I figure maybe you're doin' a number, and if you're doin' a number I figure maybe I can cool things out is all. I told 'em to take it easy with you."

The look on Kim's face was worth the price of admission.

"So I made a mistake," he went on. "You know, the way I feel about Kim and all, and so I got carried away. I never had your advantages, I never went to college, never joined a fraternity, I'm just your ordinary guy, works hard all his life and tries to make a go of it."

"You were also born stupid. Don't forget that."

"Well, I never said I was the brightest guy in the world. Just your average Joe." He gave his shoulders a shrug. He had a lot of shoulders and they moved impressively. "Look," he said, "I'm the kind of guy gives credit where credit's due. I had you wrong. You're okay. I made a mistake." He extended a paw like an overtrained retriever. "No hard feelings, huh?"

"None at all," I said, and I extended my hand and moved toward him, and for some odd reason or other my hand kept going right on past his hand, fingers bunched and rigid, and the fingers jabbed him almost exactly three inches north of his navel, assuming he was born once and had one, and that's where the solar plexus is supposed to be, and that's where his was, and I'll be damned if it didn't work like a charm.

He doubled up and turned sort of orange, and he started folding inward like a dying accordion, and I interlaced my fingers and cupped the back of his head with both hands and helped him fold up, and at the same time I raised my right knee as high as it would go, and it couldn't go all the way up because it met his face coming down.

You wouldn't believe the sound it made.

After Wong sponged the blood off him, we put him in a chair, and I stood in front of him trying not to look at his nose. It was a pleasure not to look at it.

"No hard feelings," I said, "but I've had a yen to do that since I first saw you. It was the sort of yen that kept getting stronger until there was just no restraining myself. Do you

140

understand what I'm saying, or should I use smaller words?"

He tried to glare at me.

"Here's the point," I said. "I have a feeling I'm going to get that yen over and over. It's not the sort of thing you do once and get bored with. So it would probably be a good idea if you arranged your life so that you and I were not in the same place at the same time, because kicking the shit out of you could get to be a habit with me.

"I'll tell you something else. You don't give a shit about Kim, beyond the fact that she's easy to look at and worth a couple of million dollars. She's far too good for you, and even you must be bright enough to realize that. She would have written you off a long time ago, but she was afraid of you. I think she can see that you're nothing much to be afraid of. You're not going to see Kim any more."

He tried a little harder to glare at me.

"You didn't beat me up to keep me away from Kim. You had your buddies work me over to keep me off your back, because you've got a nice little hustle going and you figured I might turn it up. I did. We got a call just before you got here today. It was from — never mind who it was from. You take days off from the docks now and then. You have one talent on God's earth: you can start a car without the key, and that's what you've been doing for a living. I could tell you just where you drive them, and just how much you get for them, but you already know. Or maybe you write the address on your shirt cuff so you won't forget it."

"Who told you?"

"Mr. Haig has some very good friends. Mr. Haig's friend asked that his name not be mentioned so I'm not going to mention it. Mr. Haig's friend asked if he could take care of this for us. He said a good friend of his has a paving contract up in Rockland County. He wanted to know if we wanted him to arrange to tuck you under a section of four-lane divided highway."

His face got very white. Except for around the nose, where it was still doing a little low-grade bleeding.

"We told him you weren't worth the trouble. If you start

being worth the trouble, meaning if you turn up on Kim's doorstep again, Mr. Haig will call him and say he changed his mind. A lot of this man's friends are in the highway construction business. I guess it's profitable."

"You son of a bitch," he said.

"I'm not finished. I'm also supposed to tell you that the auto theft people don't want to work with you any more. And that you may have a certain amount of trouble getting picked in the dock shape-up. People may tend to overlook you. You think I'm bluffing, don't you? Mr. Haig's friend didn't want his name mentioned, but there was another name he told me to mention to you."

I did so, and I never thought four syllables could have such an effect. He did everything but die on the spot.

I said, "I think you should go away now."

He went away.

So did the rest of them, ultimately. They had questions, most of them, and Haig answered them. He got into a long psychoanalytical rap with Andrea Sugar, who turned out to be very knowledgeable on Jungian psychology.

Madam Juana took him aside and told him something, and kissed his cheek, and Haig went beet-red. He had never done this before in my presence. I can't swear to what she said to him, but I can make a guess based on my instincts and my experience, because before his blush had a chance to fade she came over to me and gave me a kiss on the cheek and whispered in my ear, and what she whispered was, "You a wonnerful boy and you get the bom who kill my Maria, and anytime you wanna girl you come down and I give you best inna house, no charge, anytime you wanna fock."

Eventually Kim was the only one left. I took her upstairs and showed her the fish. She was very interested. She was also still a little nervous, so I waved at Haig and took her back to her apartment.

"I never thought you were violent, Chip. I thought of you as, you know, gentle and sensitive and aware."

142

Like the actor who turned out to be a faggot, I thought.

"And Gordie is so big and strong—"

"Well, Wong Fat showed me how to do a few things. I'm basically a very non-violent person. The only time I ever had to hit anybody was when I was a deputy sheriff in South Carolina."

"A what?"

"It was an honorary position, basically. What it came down to was that I was a bouncer in a, well, in a whorehouse, if you want to know. Sometimes guys would get drunk and pull knives, and I would have to hit 'em upside the head with this club they gave me."

"Upside the head?"

"The local expression."

"You really didn't go to college, did you?"

"I told you. I had to drop out of high school. My parents were sort of high-class con men, although I didn't know it at the time, and they got caught, and they killed themselves, and Upper Valley threw me out a few months before graduation. They were all heart."

She looked at me with those wide eyes. "You've really lived," she said.

"Well, I tend to keep moving."

"I've never met anyone like you before, Chip."

So that's about it. Ferdinand Bell is wearing a straitjacket, and will spend what's left of his life in a cell with spongy walls. This infuriates Haig, who would like to see the return of public hanging. We still haven't spawned the African gouramis, but John LiCastro finally got the results he wanted, and has a whole twenty-nine-gallon tank full of baby discus fish. Haig went over to see them the other day and says they're doing fine, and that you would have thought LiCastro had fathered them himself, the way he was carrying on.

Gordie McLeod hasn't been heard from. He never turned up to take his stuff out of Kim's apartment, and a couple of days ago I got all his things together and tucked them neatly into the incinerator. Kim said that wasn't very nice, and I said it was too bad.

I ran into Andrea Sugar at the funeral for the Vandivers. She volunteered to teach Kim the art of massage. I sort of sidestepped that one. It was probably just a nice gesture on her part, but she may have had an ulterior motive. I have nothing against lesbians, but I wouldn't want my girl to marry one.

What else? Addison Shivers called the other day. He sent a check around, and Haig returned it, and the old gentleman was displeased.

"I have not earned it, sir," Haig told him. "You hired me to look out for the interests of the late Cyrus Trelawney. I exerted myself enough to justify retaining the advances I received from yourself and Mrs. Vandiver, but I cannot say that I did much for Cyrus Trelawney, certainly not enough to warrant my accepting additional payment."

They talked some more, and an hour later the check arrived again. A messenger brought it and he tried to deliver it downstairs, which confused the girls. No one had ever tried to pay by check before. This particular check was for five thousand dollars, and it was no longer payment for work performed. Instead it was an advance against work to be performed. Because Haig had been rehired to look out for the interests of Cyrus Trelawney. Specifically, he's going to prove that Ferdinand Bell's mother was nutty as a Mars bar, and the killer wasn't Trelawney's son in the first place.

Which means I'll be making a trip to Lyons Falls before very long. I can't say I'm looking forward to it, if you want to know. The heat wave just broke and New York is not a bad place to be.

Haig has been driving me crazy lately. He keeps handing me furniture catalogues and asking me to pick out the kind of bed I like best. He won't give up, he's as single-minded as Cato on the subject of Carthage. So far I've been stubborn and have gone on paying the rent on my furnished room.

Which is probably silly. I've been spending most of my nights on Bethune Street lately, anyway.

144